'What's the matter, Miss Haydon? Disappointed because I don't fall at your feet, like all the other admirers a beautiful girl like you must have collected?'

Sara retorted resentfully, 'You make me sound the kind of female who's nothing but a man-hunter!'

'Basically, that's what all women are.'

'Well, I'm not,' she contradicted, annoyed by his cynicism. 'I'm not the slightest bit interested in adding you to my collection, as you elegantly put it. I did want to be friends, which is apparently an impossibility as far as you're concerned.'

David leaned forward to grasp her wrist. 'You're quite right. So you can forget your feminine wiles when I'm around; it would be a shame to waste them.'

*Books you will enjoy
by SANDRA FIELD*

HAPPY ENDING

'It would do you all the good in the world to fall in love.' But Nicola had no intention of doing anything of the kind, despite the insidious attractions of her neighbour, Trent Livingstone. In any case, he seemed to value his privacy as much as she—though it appeared for very different reasons. . .

SAFETY IN NUMBERS

Josh MacNeill wasn't conceited, but he knew there were plenty of women around who would be happy to have him as a husband. So what was he doing hankering after a woman who had hated him when she was ten years old and didn't seem to have changed her mind since? She wasn't the sort of wife he had in mind at all. . .

TO TRUST MY LOVE

BY
SANDRA FIELD

MILLS & BOON LIMITED
ETON HOUSE 18–24 PARADISE ROAD
RICHMOND SURREY TW9 1SR

All the characters in this book have no existence outside the imagination of the Author, and have no relation whatsoever to anyone bearing the same name or names. They are not even distantly inspired by any individual known or unknown to the Author, and all the incidents are pure invention.

All rights reserved. The text of this publication or any part thereof may not be reproduced or transmitted in any form or by any means, electronic or mechanical, including photocopying, recording, storage in an information retrieval system, or otherwise, without the written permission of the publisher.

This book is sold subject to the condition that it shall not, by way of trade or otherwise, be lent, resold, hired out or otherwise circulated without the prior consent of the publisher in any form of binding or cover other than that in which it is published and without a similar condition including this condition being imposed on the subsequent purchaser.

*First published in Great Britain 1974
by Mills & Boon Limited*

© Sandra Field 1974

*Australian copyright 1992
Philippine copyright 1992
This edition 1992*

ISBN 0 263 77438 4

*Set in Plantin 10 on 11 pt.
01-9202-52256*

Typeset in Great Britain by County Typesetters, Kent

Made and printed in Great Britain

CHAPTER ONE

SARA hesitated outside the closed door, the letter of resignation clenched in one hand, her other hand nervously smoothing the skirt of her pink uniform. Uneasily she wondered if she was doing the right thing. How much easier it would be to shirk the decision, tear up her resignation and go back to work! If only she had some sort of a definite plan for the future, instead of just a frantic desire to escape from the present, from the treadmill of repetitious days and lonely evenings. . . Coward! she scolded. Oblivious of the curious glance of a nurse who rustled past, she took a deep breath and resolutely tapped on the door.

'Come in. Oh, hello, Sara. What can I do for you?'

Holding tight to her dwindling courage, Sara silently passed the letter to her superior and sank into the straight-backed chair that faced the cluttered desk.

Miss Rutherford tore open the envelope and read the briefly worded note it contained, then leaned over the desk, her kind face mirroring the concern she felt for the slim pale girl opposite her. 'We'd be sorry to lose you, Sara, you're a very valuable member of our staff and an excellent physiotherapist. And you have a particularly good rapport with the children. It was your idea, wasn't it, that the girls working in the children's wards wear coloured uniforms, rather than the inevitable white? A small thing, I suppose, but it did make the place look a little brighter.' She paused and thoughtfully re-read the letter. 'But I've been worried about you for some time now, and I think a complete change would do you good.

Tell me, what are your plans?'

Sara answered the head of the department with her usual honesty. 'I simply don't know, Miss Rutherford.' Her slender fingers moved restlessly in her lap as she continued, 'I've enjoyed working for you. I'm sure you realise that, but things have been rather difficult lately and I would like to get away. There's Uncle Matthew's death—I can't seem to come to terms with that. He was almost like a father to me. Besides, I'm getting far too fond of some of the children here, and yet it's hard to be cheerful with them when I feel so mixed up myself.' She grimaced wryly. 'I know no good therapist becomes too deeply involved with any of her patients. I used to be able to be detached and objective, but now I'm taking the problems home with me, and worrying about them. All in all, I think I really need something different, away from sick and crippled children.' Her voice quivered. 'I'm just tired out, Miss Rutherford.'

The older woman nodded her understanding. 'You haven't looked well lately, Sara; I've been meaning to have a word with you.' Her forehead creased in thought. 'You've nothing at all in mind?'

Sara replied slowly, 'Well, there are two positions advertised in Nova Scotia, but they're both for the autumn and that seemed a long time to wait. Perhaps I can find something temporary for the summer.'

Miss Rutherford suddenly sat up straight in her chair. 'Why, Sara, I believe I've just had an inspiration!' she exclaimed. 'I was talking to my brother the day before yesterday, and he and his wife are wanting a girl to look after their two children—I'm certain he said from June until September. They have a summer home on the beach near Rocky Cape, in the Maritimes—it's a beautiful spot. Shall I phone him and see if he's found anyone yet?'

The phrase 'summer home on the beach' fell like music on Sara's ears; she had lived by the sea for six happy years. Carried along by her superior's enthusiasm, she nodded eagerly. 'Please do.'

Miss Rutherford dialled rapidly. 'May I speak to Mr Rutherford, please?. . . Harold, it's Margaret. Sorry to bother you at work. Are you still looking for someone for the summer. . .? You are? Marvellous, I think I have just the person for you. She's here now, a Miss Sara Haydon. She's a member of my staff, and one I'd highly recommend. . . Just a minute, I'll check. Sara, could you meet him for lunch tomorrow?'

Sara mesmerised, nodded again.

'Yes, she can. . .fine. I do hope you can come to an arrangement. . . That's quite all right, a pleasure. I'll see you on the weekend. Goodbye.' With a wide smile of satisfaction, she replaced the receiver. 'Harold will meet you at noon tomorrow, at Chez Pierre, it's only a block from here. His wife is away, by the way, visiting her parents in Ottawa. This might be exactly what you're looking for, Sara. My brother will fill in the details for you, and I won't do anything about your resignation until you've decided what to do.'

Somewhat incoherently, Sara thanked the department head for her help, and left the office, dazed by the speed with which her prospects had changed. Half an hour ago she had been depressed and unsure about the future, and now she couldn't suppress a flutter of anticipation as she wondered what tomorrow would bring.

It turned out to be a perfect May day, mild with a gentle spring breeze. As Sara left the hospital and walked down the bustling Montreal street, more than one pair of male eyes lingered on her charming face, with its long dark brown hair, beautifully marked brows, and grey eyes the colour of an ocean storm. She was wearing a smart red coat with black accessories, and had pulled her hair back in a smooth chignon. It had been a rush after working all morning to change and do her hair, but as she entered the elegantly appointed foyer of the French restaurant and looked uncertainly around her, she was glad she had taken the trouble.

A heavy-set man in his early forties, whose immaculately tailored suit spoke unobtrusively of wealth, turned towards her, hand outstretched. 'Miss Haydon? Harold Rutherford; I'm very pleased to meet you. Let me take your coat. If you'll come this way, I believe our table is ready.' In swift, colloquial French, which she had difficulty following, he and the waiter dealt with the menu, and two glasses of sherry appeared with miraculous speed. 'Your health, Miss Haydon. Do you mind if I talk while we eat? Time's a bit limited, I'm afraid. I have an appointment after lunch.'

As they started their chilled soup, which to Sara, at least, was a wonderful change from institutional food, Mr Rutherford explained what be required of her should she take the job. 'We go to Rocky Cape in June, as soon as the children have finished school. Stephen is eight and Patricia five; they both love the place, so I don't think you'd find any trouble keeping them amused.'

He was interrupted by the arrival of their main course, a steaming and fragrant lobster Newburg, served with rice and a crisp salad. Sara smiled at her companion. 'Doesn't that look delicious? I grew up by the sea, Mr Rutherford, and the first lobster of the season was always an event. We'd cook it in salt water, and eat it warm from the shell, dipped in melted butter. Food fit for the gods!'

Harold Rutherford laughed. 'You would feel very much at home at the Cape, then; we always have one or two lobster boils a summer.' While they ate, he continued, 'There are really two reasons why we need someone. Both my wife Marilyn and I are avid golfers, so whenever weather permits we spend the whole day on the course; it's one of the best in Canada, by the way. And secondly, I have to make the occasional trip to Montreal to keep an eye on my business interests, and frequently Marilyn accompanies me. We do have a full-time housekeeper, Mrs Donnelly; she gets the meals and keeps the house running smoothly. Your only responsibility would be the children, they're just too young to be running around the beach and cliffs by themselves. Marilyn's little car would be available for you to take them on picnics and excursions to the lakes and playgrounds in the area. Most of your evenings would be free, and at least one day a week. You'd have your own room, and the place is big enough to give you privacy when you want it.' He paused. 'I'd better give you the disadvantages too. We're very isolated: the nearest city is a hundred miles away, the nearest town of any size fifty miles. There's a decided dearth of sophistication and night life—a couple of restaurants, one discothèque and a resort hotel are about it.' He looked questioningly at Sara. 'It depends what you're looking for; if it's bright lights, Rocky Cape is the wrong place. If it's peace and quiet, and a chance to enjoy the woods and beaches— well, I'd recommend it.'

For a moment Sara was silent, her face distressed. She liked this genial man, and felt he should know a little of her background. Picking her words with care, she said, 'Mr Rutherford, I think I ought to explain why I'm interested in this job. Do you mind listening to a bit of my past history?'

'Please go ahead. To be frank, I am rather curious. Rocky Cape is a long way from Montreal, and I don't mean only in terms of miles.'

'I was born in England. My mother died when I was

three, and my father died eleven years ago, my only other relative was a widowed uncle here in Canada. I lived with Uncle Matthew for six years, and came to love him dearly; he took the unexpected arrival of a twelve-year-old quite in his stride. When I was eighteen, I went away to study physiotherapy, and then was lucky enough to get my present job; but I always spent my long weekends and holidays with him. He suffered from arthritis all the time I knew him, that was what led to my interest in physiotherapy.'

She remembered how, more than once, she had been tempted to give up her therapy course, and stay home to look after him. 'No,' he had insisted, 'I want you to finish your training, Sara. Naturally I hope you'll get married and raise a family—but all women should have a career to fall back on, life's an uncertain business.' Perhaps even then he had had a premonition of the shortness of his own future. . .

Her voice shook as she said, 'He had a fatal heart attack four weeks ago. I'd visited him shortly beforehand at Easter, and when I got the telegram, I couldn't believe he was dead. He'd been so full of plans for the summer; I was going to spend most of July with him. After the funeral, I closed up the old house and came back to Montreal; it seemed the logical thing to do. Then I caught 'flu and couldn't seem to shake it, and since then I feel as though I'm stifling in the city; Uncle Matthew's house overlooked the sea in a tiny village on the south shore of Nova Scotia.' She regained her self-control and continued with assurance, 'No, I'm not looking for bright lights, far from it. Besides, I'm very fond of children; for over a year now I've had a complete responsibility for the children's wards. In fact, your sister claims that my main fault is becoming too involved with them.'

She smiled apologetically at the man opposite her. 'I'm sorry to burden you with my life story, but you can see why your offer is so providential for me.'

Her companion nodded sympathetically. 'Yes, I do see that. But perhaps you'd prefer a day or two to think about it, before you decide. I assure you that references won't be needed; my sister's recommendation is high praise indeed.' He smiled at Sara's quick flush of pleasure. 'There is one other thing I must bring up. A good friend of ours, a bachelor by the name of David Ramsay, stays near us, about a mile up the beach. His nephew Timothy, who's an orphan and a little younger than Stephen, lives with him. In fact, David is Timothy's guardian. The two boys are close friends, and I imagine a good many days you'd have three children on your hands, rather than two.'

Sara laughed. 'Mr Rutherford, I frequently have a dozen on my hands, and sick ones at that. Timothy wouldn't pose a problem at all. And there's no question of my decision—I would be very happy to come to Rocky Cape and look after the children.'

Harold Rutherford was clearly delighted, and raising his glass, he proposed a toast: 'Let's drink to a good summer, Miss Haydon.'

Over coffee and liqueurs, he finalised salary arrangements, her arrival date and transport. 'After you leave the train at Saraguay, I'm afraid the final hundred miles have to be covered in a rather rattletrap old bus; there are usually only five or six passengers, so the company doesn't go in for modernity. You can get off at the end of our driveway, and we'll meet you there. Here's my office phone number in case you have any questions between now and then.'

He helped her on with her coat, and a few minutes later said goodbye to her on the crowded pavement, raising his hat with old-fashioned politeness. Sara hurried back to the hospital, trying to sort out her impressions. Harold Rutherford was a pleasant man, and she would have to hope that his wife and family were the same. Whatever happened, at least she would be able to get her life back in perspective to the sound of ocean waves and the tang of salt air, rather than rushing traffic and choking exhaust fumes.

The next four weeks were busy ones for her, giving her scant opportunity to brood over her grief. Her workload at the hospital was exceptionally heavy, or perhaps Miss Rutherford was purposely filling every minute of her day. Off duty she was equally occupied. She had taken out last summer's wardrobe and spread it on her bed—a few faded cotton dresses and some well-worn trousers and shorts. How shabby they looked! She hadn't spent much money on clothes lately; since starting to work, she'd sent every penny she could spare to her uncle, to supplement his pension. Wearing last year's dresses had been a small price to pay for the knowledge that he could at last afford a few extras. But now, of course, her money was her own, and if this lonely thought brought tears there was no one there to see them.

She was an expert seamstress, and spent an entire Saturday shopping for materials and patterns. That evening she cleared her kitchen table and started cutting out a sundress. Utterly absorbed, the ring of the doorbell a couple of hours later took her by surprise. She opened the door and smiled at the willowy and attractive girl standing there. 'Oh, hello, Joan, come in. Ignore the mess, please!'

Joan Madison was a nurse on the surgical ward and had been a close friend of Sara's for over a year. Expensively dressed and exquisitely groomed, engaged to a well-to-do business executive, Joan had always taken the luxuries of life for granted before she met Sara. She deeply admired the latter's cheerfulness and courage under very straitened circumstances, and now she sighed with envy at her industry. 'You sew so beautifully, I wish I had your patience. Mmm, gorgeous material too. What else are you going to make?'

While Sara put on a pot of coffee, Joan's eyes surveyed the bare little room, and dwelt affectionately on her friend's quiet, pale features. She knew she would miss the younger girl's companionship, but she was unselfishly pleased that a change had come into Sara's life, and that she had the chance of a carefree and relatively lazy summer. She worked much too hard. And, Joan hoped, perhaps this summer her friend would meet a man who would bring her lasting happiness, and make her forget the basic loneliness and lack of security that lay beneath her tranquil exterior. Poor Sara. . .her mother, her father, her uncle—one by one they had died, and left her alone, Joan thought of her own parents and the host of aunts, uncles and cousins scattered across the width of Canada. Maybe she didn't see some of them very often, but nevertheless it was good to know they were there.

'You're really happy to get away from Montreal, aren't you, Sara?' she asked.

'Yes, I am, Joan. No reflection on you, I'm going to miss you. But if Rocky Cape is half as nice as it sounds, it will be like going home. We lived in a small village in England, and you've been to my uncle's—no one would call it the hub of civilisation!'

Joan chuckled. 'Remember when I wanted you to go skiing in the Laurentians with Simon and me, and Tom Hadley? I couldn't see why you'd pass up a weekend like that to visit a mere uncle! Well, I understand now. You must be glad you visited him as much as you did.'

Sara nodded soberly. 'Yes, I certainly am. Here, your

coffee's getting cold. Sugar?'

'No, have to watch my figure. Just a little milk. Thanks, Sara.' She changed the subject. 'At least you aren't leaving behind a favourite young man.'

'You and Simon did your best to find me one, didn't you? Think of all those wasted double dates!' She put her head to one side in perplexity. 'They were pleasant enough men in their own way, Joan. But they all seemed to have a veneer of ruthlessness as far as their jobs and friends were concerned; they were very busy looking after number one! I couldn't imagine falling in love with any of them. Anyway, I object to fending off advances in the back seat of a taxi!'

Joan grinned. 'You shouldn't look so fragile and feminine, then. You have to get tough with fellows like that.'

Sara crinkled her nose in thought, wanting Joan to understand what had been missing in those casual dates. 'I didn't seem to talk the same language as any of them. I do enjoy some aspects of city life, but basically I'll always be an outdoors person—everything seems simpler in the country somehow. If I'm offered the choice of a nightclub or a walk along the beach, I'll take the beach any day. Which, I suppose, is why I jumped at this job with the Rutherfords.'

'Well, my country cousin,' teased Joan, 'you'll have to put up with one more outing with Simon and me; we're taking you out for dinner your last evening here.'

Almost before Sara knew it, that last evening was upon her. Her final day at the hospital had been a long and rather difficult one. She had said goodbye to all the children under her care, wondering if she would ever see any of them again, and yet able to joke with them and leave them laughing. There was a lump in her throat as she accepted the parting gift from the girls in her department, an intricately knitted Aran pullover. She had dreaded the last interview with Miss Rutherford, unnecessarily so as it turned out. 'I won't say goodbye, Sara, I'll be keeping in touch with you through my brother, and who knows, I may take a few days later on to visit you all up there. Have a good summer, my dear. Put on a little weight and get some colour in your cheeks.' And with genuine affection, she lightly kissed the girl on the cheek.

The warmth of this gesture stayed with Sara through the long and often tedious train journey, and the taxi ride from a dirty railway station to an equally dirty bus terminal. As she bought her ticket, she caught sight of the 'rattletrap' bus, and giggled to herself at the aptness of Mr Rutherford's description. It seated about a dozen, was painted in violent shades of blue and green, and waited with what was surely an air of patient suffering for its journey to begin. And begin it did, with a clashing of gears and a series of defiant backfires. Gradually Sara became accustomed to the jolting method of progress; the city was left behind, the countryside unfolded in gently rolling hills, and she even started to enjoy the drive.

It was broken halfway by a short ferry ride across an inlet of the sea. As the boat pulled away from the dock, waves slapping against its prow, Sara took a deep breath of the fresh salt air, and stretched her cramped limbs. The sun glinted on the water, and the wind tugged at her hair, blowing loose tendrils across her face. Surely in these beautiful surroundings she could throw off her unhappiness. If only she weren't so alone—she belonged to no one now. . . Firmly she thrust these desolate thoughts away, straightened her slender shoulders, and forced herself to concentrate on the spruce-clad hills and the curve of the sandbar as they approached the opposite shore.

She climbed back in her seat again and the bus trundled protestingly off the ferry and up the hill. Fatigue washed over her, so she closed her eyes, dozing fitfully until the driver's voice roused her with a start. 'Your stop next, miss. Just half a mile further.'

She hurriedly smoothed her hair and reapplied her lipstick, feeling her stomach tighten with sudden apprehension as the bus creaked to a halt; three figures were waiting for her on the side of the road. The driver swung down her luggage, and she turned to meet Harold Rutherford. He greeted her with genuine pleasure. 'Delighted to see you again, Miss Haydon. These are our children, Patricia and Stephen.'

Sara looked at the two small faces upturned to hers, and a smile tugged at her lips when she said hello to them. Harold picked up her suitcases and she was ruefully conscious of their shabbiness in contrast to his sharply creased trousers and gleaming leather shoes. Stephen grabbed the duffel bag, and, seeing disappointment cloud Patricia's brown eyes, Sara asked, 'Would you mind carrying my handbag, Patricia? It's rather heavy.' She was repaid by a gap-toothed grin, and the four of them started down the gravel driveway, Sara recounting her impressions of the bus to her amused companion.

They wound their way through sweetly scented woods of pine and spruce; when they turned the last corner to come in sight of the house, the girl gave a gasp of pure delight. 'Oh, Mr Rutherford, it's beautiful!' she exclaimed impulsively, and stood still a minute, drinking in the peaceful scene. The house was built of mellow brick with double chimneys and a grey slate roof; smooth green lawn separated it from a grove of spruces, the sandbar and the sparkling ocean.

Harold Rutherford was obviously pleased with her

reaction. 'You can see why we spend every summer here,' he said. 'Come in and meet my wife.' He pushed open the heavy oak front door and ushered her into a room that harmoniously combined luxury with comfort. 'Marilyn, we're back. Oh, there you are. This is Miss Haydon. Sara, my wife Marilyn.'

Marilyn Rutherford must have been ten years younger than her husband, small and plump, with a vivacious face and glossy auburn curls. She held out her hand in greeting. 'Good afternoon, Miss Haydon. We're very happy to have you. I've heard glowing reports of you from my husband's sister; you have quite a reputation to keep up!'

Her smile was so genuinely friendly that Sara felt a prickle of tears at the back of her eyes. 'You make me feel very welcome, Mrs Rutherford,' she said, a slight tremor of weariness in her voice.

With quick intuition, Marilyn replied, 'Let me show you your room. You'll probably want to rest for a while before dinner.' She led Sara down a long carpeted hallway, and opened the end door, explaining apologetically that the room was rather small but did have its own bathroom.

The sun was shining through the bedroom window and the breeze ruffled the crisp blue curtains. The furniture was early Canadian: a white-painted spool bed covered with a brightly patterned home-made quilt, a pine dresser, and an old-fashioned hand-carved rocking chair. Hooked rugs were scattered on the gleaming hardwood floor, and shells from the beach decorated the bookshelves. A small door led to the compact and gaily painted bathroom.

To Sara, who for the past two years had occupied a small room in the old hospital residence, with institutional furniture and a view of the adjoining brick building, it was perfect, and her smile was radiant as she turned to Mrs Rutherford. 'I've never had such a beautiful room.'

Surprised admiration crossed Marilyn's face, but Sara was unaware of how happiness lit up her deep grey eyes, and gave her an appealing beauty.

Harold Rutherford came down the hall with her cases, and his wife urged, 'Please, Miss Haydon, just make yourself at home. There's lots of hot water any time you want a bath. We'll have dinner in an hour, I'll call you when it's ready.'

Sara murmured her thanks and was left alone. She crossed to the window, and surveyed the vista of beach and sea, the only sounds were the ripple of a stream in the nearby woods, and the distant rhythm of the waves. Her fascinated gaze returned to the room, and she suddenly noticed its single painting on the opposite wall over her bed: rust-red and gold chrysanthemums in a blue pottery vase glowed against the dark background, and something within her responded to its colour and vitality. Her apprehension faded; she sang softly to herself as she filled the bath with steaming water and soaked the strain out of her tired muscles. Afterwards, she slipped on a simple tangerine linen dress, brushed her dark hair until it shone, and pulled it back with a bright silk scarf. When Mrs Rutherford tapped at her door a few minutes later, Sara felt relaxed and capable of dealing with anything.

The meal was beautifully prepared; the conversation flowed easily over Sara's trip, the Montreal shops and theatres, a controversial best-seller they all had read. A fire crackled cheerfully in the fireplace, and through the wide picture window, darkness fell over the sea, and the first stars shone.

'The children are eating with Mrs Donnelly, our

housekeeper, this evening,' Marilyn explained. 'I thought a little peace and quiet might be in order after your long journey, and you'll have lots of time to get acquainted with them tomorrow. Let's have our coffee around the fire, Harold.' After they were settled in deep armchairs, she went on, 'We feel very lucky to have you here for the summer, Miss Haydon; but perhaps I may call you Sara?'

'Please do. In fact, I was wondering if you'd mind if the children call me by my first name, when we get to know each other? "Miss Haydon" seems a bit formal, when I'm going to be with them so much.'

Marilyn nodded in agreement. 'That would be fine. And we're Marilyn and Harold to you. By the way, do I detect a trace of English accent?'

'Yes, I was born in Cornwall. I love this country now, but I suppose I'll always have a soft spot for England, and certain things still make me miss it: daffodils growing wild under the trees, and the scent of honeysuckle—it grew over the hedgerows near my home.'

She looked up inquiringly as Marilyn chuckled. 'There, Harold, someone else will enjoy our honeysuckle. We have it growing on the old stone wall behind the vegetable garden, Sara. Harold was convinced it wouldn't survive the Canadian winters, but I knew better.' And as she glanced teasingly at her husband, and he ruffled her red curls, it was obvious that they adored each other.

Sara felt a pang of envy at their closeness; would she ever love a man, and be loved in return like that? An image of the painting on her wall flashed across her mind; its warmth and colour had soothed her fear and loneliness like the hand of love. Suddenly curious, she remarked, 'I was admiring the painting in my room,

Mr Rutherford; who is the artist?'

'You must by psychic, Sara,' he smiled in reply. 'I was just thinking about him. You remember I mentioned Timothy, Stephen's friend. His uncle, David Ramsay, who is also his guardian, painted that picture several years ago. In fact, it would have been while Tim's father and mother were living. David's a professor of English at the university in Rochford, so of course his summers are free of lectures, and he spends as much time as he can at the Cape—he should be arriving in about a week. Perhaps I'd better tell you a little about Tim, because you'll probably be seeing quite a bit of him. His parents were killed in a car accident three years ago, when Tim was four. David was named guardian in the will; at the time he was engaged to be married, so this seemed a good arrangement. Linda, his fiancée, was a beautiful girl, from a well known and extremely wealthy Ottawa family, and they were very much in love. Nobody seems to know what happened next—it's a real mystery. All of a sudden the engagement was off, Linda went back to Ottawa, and David would never discuss it. But he insisted on keeping Tim, even though the grandmother would have taken him. And they certainly get along well together. David finished that painting and gave it to us shortly after he met Linda; it was love at first sight with those two. He withdrew into himself after they separated, and as far as I know, he's done very little painting since then. So we moved it from the dining-room into the spare room; he drops in quite frequently, you see, and we didn't want to remind him of happier days.' He smiled affectionately at his wife. 'That was Marilyn's reasoning, anyway. She insisted that Timothy needs a mother, but you wouldn't dare suggest that to David, he'd bite your head off.'

Sara nodded, her grey eyes sad. 'Yes, a child needs a

mother. I'll be very happy to help out with Tim in any way I can.'

They fell silent, gazing into the dancing flames; finally Sara stirred in her chair and got to her feet. 'Will you excuse me, please? It's been a long day, and I want to be wide awake in the morning.' Shyly she continued, 'I'd like to thank you both for making me so welcome. Goodnight.'

She left them by the fire, and went to her room. As she drew the curtains, she contemplated the vivid flowers over her bed. She had been right, they did glow with the warmth of love, but it was a love that had not survived. It had withered like the real flowers. She wondered why, curious to meet this David Ramsay.

Slowly she finished unpacking, putting her clothes neatly in the lavender-scented drawers, and arranging her few favourite books on the shelves. She smiled fondly at the framed photograph of her parents, and at the snapshot of Uncle Matthew, his shaggy white head outlined against the empty sky. He would feel at home in this place. And tomorrow she would get to know the children. . .she fell asleep to the murmur of the waves on the shore.

CHAPTER TWO

SARA awoke early the next morning with an anticipation for the day ahead that she hadn't experienced for several weeks. Dressed in jeans and a long-sleeved gingham shirt, she made her way to the kitchen. 'Good morning, Mrs Donnelly; hello, Patricia and Stephen.'

The housekeeper was a cheery middle-aged woman, a marvel of efficiency, who nevertheless always had time for 'a cup of tea with my feet up.' Putting down a bowl of steaming oatmeal, she advised, 'Eat up, Miss Sara, you young things are too thin these days.'

'Mmm, thank you, that looks delicious.' Helping herself to brown sugar, Sara grinned conspiratorially at the children. 'Will you show me around this morning? It's such a lovely day, I can't wait to explore.'

Stephen nodded vigorously. He was a friendly and outgoing boy, with his mother's dark red hair, and a liberal sprinkling of freckles. His sister, in contrast, was quiet and self-contained, and her large brown eyes regarded Sara gravely. 'This is Miss Moppet,' she stated, indicating a floppy rag doll by her plate. 'She goes everywhere I go.'

Sara had always had an empathy for children, and they were chattering freely together as they pulled on jackets and went out into the crisp June air.

'I think she should meet Lady and Benedict first, don't you, Patricia?' demanded Stephen, taking charge of the expedition.

'Here's Lady now,' cried the little girl, running to hug the sedate golden retriever who came round the corner of the house, tail waving serenely.

'Benedict's probably still in the kennel, we'll let him out. He's only seven months old, and Daddy says he's obstreperous.' Stephen produced this big word with pride.

Benedict turned out to be a boisterous coal-black Labrador, bouncing with energy and high spirits. The five of them, plus Miss Moppet, set off in procession to view the tool shed, the vegetable garden, the budding honeysuckle on the old stone wall, and the stream in the woods with its bridge of rough-hewn planks. The children had a cache of little wooden boats there, and Sara sat on a rock with her back against a tree trunk, enjoying their absorption as they played; Stephen, who was quick and nimble, occasionally became impatient with Patricia's more deliberate ways, but at the same time Sara was quite sure he would defend her fiercely against any outsider.

After a while, they put the boats carefully back in the box, and Stephen produced a rubber ball from his pocket. 'Could we play with the dogs on the beach?' he asked hopefully. 'We're not allowed there by ourselves.'

'Let's,' said Sara happily. 'It haven't been down there yet.' They followed the stream through the shaded woods, and came out on to the dazzling sand. Even the staid Lady forgot her dignity and sprinted after the ball, while Benedict scampered madly in circles. They were all breathless and laughing when they tumbled in the back door, to be met with the tempting aroma of a chicken casserole for lunch. Sara discovered to her amazement that she was famished, and told Mrs Donnelly she couldn't remember when food had tasted so good.

While they were eating, Harold Rutherford came into the kitchen. 'Good morning, all.' He kissed his son and daughter, and grinned sheepishly at Sara. 'This is a disgraceful hour to be getting up. Knowing you were here and would keep an eye on the children, we were thoroughly lazy this morning. However, I was thinking that after lunch I could show you the gear-shift on the car; we'll take a run to the village just to make sure you've got the hang of it.'

The little car was new and shiny, and Sara had no serious trouble with it. Her eyes twinkled as she explained to her employer, 'I learned to drive on Uncle Matthew's rather disreputable old truck; I think it must have been a relative of your bus. If I could drive that, I could drive anything.'

The village was charmingly situated in a sheltered cove, and consisted of a few gaily painted houses on the green slopes, a row of fish shacks along the wharf, and a post office and general store.

When they returned, Stephen and Patricia were waiting for her on the step, obviously bursting with a plan. 'It's low tide,' began the boy. 'We could take our buckets and look for crabs and starfish in the pools.'

'Just let me get my boots,' Sara laughed. 'Is the extra bucket for me?'

The children were delighted with her ready agreement, and as Harold held the door open for her, he smiled his approval of her enthusiasm. The three of them had a wonderful time poking among the seaweed and clambering over the rocks; it was late afternoon when they trailed back to the house with their booty. Sara was well pleased with her new charges, for they were polite and well-behaved, yet each possessed a healthy spark of mischief. After supper, she was taken to inspect the playroom, where they mulled over a complicated jigsaw puzzle until bedtime, Sara herself went to bed not long afterwards, the unaccustomed fresh air sending her deeply and dreamlessly to sleep.

The days fell easily into a pattern. She and the children explored the beach and cliffs, walked the dogs, dammed the stream, and in rainy weather played Monopoly and cards in the playroom. And one evening, reflectively brushing her hair before bed, Sara realised she had been there a week. The sharp ache of Uncle Matthew's death had subsided; the look of strain was gone from her eyes, and her cheeks glowed with healthy colour. She had slipped smoothly into her niche in the Rutherford household; she was already fond of the children and knew this feeling to be reciprocal. Stephen's allegiance had been won right from the start by her genuine love of the outdoors. Shy Patricia had been won over the evening Sara patiently helped her make a new dress for Miss Moppet from some of her sewing remnants.

Her reverie was interrupted by the brisk patter of rain against the window—surely it wouldn't rain tomorrow, her first day off. The four Rutherfords were going to Saraguay for the day, to buy supplies for the party Marilyn and Harold were giving the following evening. 'Of course you're invited to it, Sara,' Marilyn had warmly insisted. 'You're one of the family now.' They had offered to take Sara into the city with them, but she preferred to have a day to herself; she had never been afraid of solitude. And besides, there were the finishing touches to put on the long skirt she was making for the party.

She needn't have worried about the weather, for although the mournful dirge of the foghorn awoke her, by mid-morning the sun had dispersed the mist, and it promised to be the warmest day so far. She completed her sewing, and even her critical eye was pleased with the result.

After lunch, she called Benedict and set off down the beach, determined to discover what was on the other side of the rocky point; she hadn't been in that direction with the children. Delighting in the dazzling white surf and gurgle of the backwash, she scrambled over the rocks, which were festooned with lank, wet seaweed, and encrusted with barnacles. Above the tide level, a few stunted spruces eked out a precarious existence on the hump-backed peninsula, and the grass was sprinkled with golden dandelions and delicate cinquefoil. Exhilarated by the long stretch of deserted beach that lay beyond, she sprinted along the hard-packed sand, and collapsed, laughing and gasping for breath, against a big boulder.

Then, out of the corner of her eye, she saw Benedict vainly chasing a flock of sparrows; he dashed over the bank and out of sight. In abrupt alarm she followed him across the dunes, eel grass whipping against her jeans, and Harold's voice echoing in her ears, '. . .oh, yes, a pure-bred, his parents were champions.' Heaven knows what he had cost! What would she do if she lost him? She noticed a path winding through the trees and ran along it, her feet soundless in the soft grass, pausing occasionally to shout, 'Ben, Ben, here, boy!' Growing thoroughly exasperated with him, pure-bred or no pure-bred, she ducked under an elder bush and rounded a dense spruce with a fresh burst of speed.

Suddenly all the breath was knocked out of her lungs, as she cannoned into the hard body of a man who had just straightened at her approach. She found herself grasped rigidly by each arm, her eyes level with a red-checked shirt, and one small part of her mind noticed that a button was missing. Stunned by the impact, fright blanching her cheeks, she encountered a pair of the bluest and angriest eyes she had ever seen.

'First your dog—I presume that ill-trained mutt is yours—now you! He woke me from the first decent sleep

I've had all week. If you're incapable of controlling an animal, you shouldn't have one.'

Even as a slightly hysterical giggle rose in her throat at the thought of Harold Rutherford's Champion Benedict being regarded as a mutt, it was quelled by the harsh resentment in this formidable stranger's face. 'I'm terribly sorry,' she stammered, a pulse beating frantically in her throat. 'He's never run away like that before.' She felt a quick concern at the lines of pain about his mouth. 'Did I hurt you?'

In a voice grating with exasperation, he rejected her faltered apology and solicitude. 'Kindly get your dog, and don't let me see him here again. This does happen to be private property, you know.'

Stung by his unyielding manner, Sara's temper flared. 'If you'd let me go,' she said icily, 'I will certainly remove both myself and my dog, and we shall be only too pleased never to lay eyes on you again!'

He released her abruptly, but her air of rather tremulous dignity was spoiled by Benedict, who came bounding out of the trees and jumped up on her, pink tongue lolling and big jaws laughing. She looked very young and appealing in her faded jeans and soft blue shirt, dark hair falling around her flushed face as she tried to fend off Ben's boisterous pleasure at seeing her again. But the austere coldness of the man's features did not soften, and she felt the prick of angry tears while she fumbled with the dog's lead.

She half-turned to reiterate her apology, but the stranger had already dismissed her, and was picking up his cigarettes from the ground. Her legs trembling, she walked slowly back towards the beach, Benedict pacing sedately beside her. 'You wretched animal, you're on your best behaviour now that it's too late,' she scolded. She was sure she'd never met such an arrogant, insufferable male; he didn't have to be so rude just because his precious sleep had been disturbed—the incident, after all, had had its comic side. She mentally vowed to avoid this part of the beach for the rest of her stay.

By the time she reached home, she had managed to regain her usual equanimity. But for some reason she didn't mention the occurrence to the Rutherfords when they returned, and she found it difficult to sleep that night: hard blue eyes, and broad shoulders in a shirt that needed mending, kept intruding on her vision.

The next day, she was too busy to dwell on the incident, for the house was humming with preparations for the party, and as usual, the children claimed a good bit of her time. But by early evening, everything was under control, and she and Marilyn were able to relax by the fire for a few minutes. Despite their differences, a deepening friendship had sprung up between them, and they chatted casually together, Marilyn mentioning the names of some of the expected guests. 'I don't want you to be overwhelmed by strangers,' she assured Sara. 'Oh, I know what I meant to tell you. David Ramsay and Timothy arrived a couple of days ago—Harold was talking to them today at the post office. I expect David will be along later. They had a most unfortunate car accident about a month ago; another of those wretched drunken drivers. David got away with bruised ribs and a concussion, but poor Tim is in a cast, his leg was broken. Perhaps tomorrow he could come here for a while to play with Stephen.'

'What a shame! Of course he could.'

'Heavens, we'd better get dressed!' Marilyn exclaimed. 'The Campbells are always early.'

Unsuccessfully, Sara tried to suppress her excitement as she skilfully arranged her shining hair on top of her head in a loose cascade of curls. It was a long time since she'd been to a party. She hoped her clothes wouldn't look home-made, for she was convinced none of the Rutherfords' friends would make their own. She need not have worried; the long, brightly patterned skirt emphasised her slimness, and the pale silk shirt set off to perfection her slender neck, with its crown of dark hair.

When she shyly re-entered the room, Harold raised his eyebrows and whistled in appreciation. 'You look a little different from the way you did playing ball on the beach in your jeans! Oh, there's the bell. Excuse me a minute, I'll get you a drink when I come back.' He returned, and introduced their first guests. 'Mr and Mrs Campbell, Miss Sara Haydon, who's staying with us for the summer. Ah, here's Marilyn. What can I get you all to drink?'

As the room gradually filled with people, Sara relaxed and found she was enjoying herself. She was soon cornered by Dr Callaghan, the genial middle-aged doctor from the small local hospital. He had been attracted to her side by her charming air of diffidence in this roomful of self-assured and wealthy guests. But when he discovered her profession, his conversation rapidly became technical, and they were deep in an involved discussion of some new types of equipment when Harold Rutherford came up behind them, accompanied by a tall, broad-shouldered man.

'Sara, may I interrupt? This is our good friend, David Ramsay.'

With interest, Sara turned to meet Tim's uncle. Her smile froze on her lips; a gasp of consternation escaped her.

David Ramsay's sea-blue eyes widened in puzzled recognition, and flickered a moment in what could have been unwilling admiration, before a concealing mask of reserve came down over his rugged face. 'Oh, yes,' he began coolly, 'we have already met, haven't we, Miss Haydon? Yesterday, was it?'

Infuriated by his effrontery, yet very conscious of her employer's eyes on them both, she managed to reply with at least a semblance of politeness, 'Yes, that's right.' She glanced at Harold. 'I'm afraid your Benedict disgraced himself by trespassing on Mr Ramsay's property.'

Fortunately for Sara, whose animosity was simmering just below the surface, Harold caught sight of Dr Callaghan's empty glass. 'Murray, you need a refill. And come and sample some of the food on the buffet.'

Sara smiled a quick goodbye at the friendly doctor, then looked up at David Ramsay, her grey eyes blazing. 'Have you posted "No Trespassing" signs yet?' His mouth tightened ominously, but before he could reply, she swept on, 'As you obviously consider me incompetent, I expect you'll want to make other arrangements for Timothy. After all, if I can't control Mr Rutherford's dog, I could hardly be entrusted with the welfare of your newphew.'

Her heart quailed momentarily as he looked daggers at her. With a visible effort, he controlled his rising anger, and his voice was exasperatingly calm and detached as he shrugged, 'One shouldn't always judge from first impressions, Miss Haydon.' Unbelievably, a quick glint of humour softened his expression. 'I think you will find Tim a little easier to manage than the dog. After all, we wouldn't want to embarrass our host and hostess, would we? Harold was very pleased that you were willing to take on an extra child. Now, if you'll excuse me, I see an old friend over there.'

Left alone, Sara put her drink down with fingers that trembled slightly. What a mix-up, just as the summer had begun so beautifully! What had she shouted at him yesterday? 'I'll be pleased never to lay eyes on you again!' And because of Tim, she thought ruefully, she'd probably be laying eyes on him several times a week. Reluctantly she had to admit that in his superbly fitting grey-blue suit, with his crisp, fair hair springing from his forehead, David Ramsay was a disturbingly handsome man. Also, she reminded herself forcefully, a very rude one. She hoped Tim wouldn't have his uncle's unpleasant ways.

Taking a grip on herself, she went to help Marilyn pass the trays of delicious, hot canapés, and the rest of the evening was uneventful, although she did have a tendency to avoid that corner of the room that contained David Ramsay. He was plainly very much at ease with these people, and seemed to be at the centre of a group whenever she looked. She heard him laugh occasionally, marvelling how young and vital he appeared without that hard mask of reticence. She was increasingly curious to meet Timothy; there was a good chance she would tomorrow. . .

In fact, it was the following afternoon that Harold Rutherford and his son went to fetch Tim in the car, Stephen jumping about impatiently at the prospect of seeing his friend again. When they returned, Sara's heart was won immediately by the thin little boy who clambered awkwardly out of the car, firmly refusing Stephen's offer of help. He had his uncle's fair hair and vivid blue eyes, and greeted Sara shyly. Stephen enthusiastically bore him away to inspect his new car racing set, Patricia and Miss Moppet trailing behind.

Harold commented to the girl, 'David was telling me that Tim's been quite nervous about being driven since the accident. But he's a brave little fellow, didn't make a sound on the way over. You'll find him quite independent; I suppose losing his parents so young made him that way.'

'Yes, it would,' Sara soberly agreed, her grey eyes momentarily lost in reminiscence. She roused herself and added, 'Well, I'd better see what's happening in the playroom; Stephen often has trouble fitting the track together.' However, when she entered the room, she was amused to notice that Stephen had left the recalcitrant track to Tim's more agile fingers. She sat quietly in a corner chair, her book in her lap, watching them as they played. The two boys were a perfect foil for each other: exuberant Stephen, such a live wire, and so quick to lose his patience; and steadfast Timothy, quiet, perservering and good-natured. Sara saw depths in him as yet undeveloped in Stephen. He was too pale, she would have to get him out in the sun more. 'How long before your cast comes off, Tim?' she interjected into a pause in the game.

'Three weeks, I think. Heavy old thing, I hate it. I can't wait to run around again.'

When they were tired of the cars, she joined them in a riotous game of Monopoly until supper time. It was dusk when Harold drove Tim home, but at breakfast the next day, Stephen and Patricia were as full of energy as ever.

'Sara, let's go to the falls today,' Stephen suggested. 'It's one of our favourite places, isn't it, Patricia? We could take our boats and play in the stream.'

'If your mother doesn't need the car, I expect we can go,' Sara agreed. 'I should think it's warm enough for us to take a picnic, if you'd like to.'

Their eager response made her laugh, and with a will all three hurried to complete their morning chores, and gathered together boots, sweaters and toys. But as Sara was carrying the picnic basket to the car, she was disconcerted to see David Ramsay arrive in an ancient jeep, Tim perched beside him. The man jumped out and lifted his nephew down, and again she felt that strong pull of attraction. What a devastatingly handsome man he was! Khaki trousers and a lumberman's jacket emphasised his splendid physique and strongly hewn features, yet, despite his size, he moved with the fluent control of an athlete.

Stephen's face fell. 'How can Tim go to the falls? He couldn't walk on the path, it's too steep.' He stood there uncertainly, torn between his desire to go, and his reluctance to disappoint his friend.

Sara was surprised by the understanding in David's voice when he asked, 'What's the matter, Stephen?'

'Sara was planning to take us to the falls, but I don't see how Tim could manage,' the boy explained, adding bravely, 'I guess we could go another day.'

'I see. I have a suggestion—why don't we all pile into the jeep, and I'll take you there. I could carry Tim down the path. That is, if Miss Haydon wouldn't mind?' His sardonic eyes dared her to protest.

How could she refuse? Sara thought irritably, watching the children's anxious faces wait for her answer. 'I'll pack a few more sandwiches,' she said ungraciously. Never had she met anyone as capable of disconcerting her as this arrogant stranger! Hurriedly adding to the picnic in the kitchen, she regained her poise, and resolved to adopt an air of calm dignity in his presence. But to her annoyance, even the touch of his hand as he helped her into the jeep was enough to set her nerves tingling.

The road to the falls was a narrow, winding track through dense forest; it climbed steadily from sea level with magnificent views of the distant ocean gleaming in the sun. The children kept their eyes peeled for wildlife, and were rewarded when David came to a halt, allowing a huge porcupine to waddle slowly across their path.

'That's why so many of them get run over,' he commented. 'I'm afraid those spines aren't much protection against a car travelling forty or fifty miles an hour.'

Humorously, Sara decided she had to give him credit for kindness to children and animals, even if he did hate women. His quick grasp of Stephen's dilemma earlier had puzzled her, for it didn't fit the mental image she had of a man who would ride roughshod over other people's feelings. She wondered why he had come today—perhaps to see if she was an acceptable companion for his nephew!

The road came to an end in a clearing, and the children scrambled out, Sara neatly avoiding David's outstretched hand. 'I'm really very independent, Mr Ramsay,' she said demurely. 'You mustn't spoil me.'

'In that case, perhaps you could carry the basket while I take Tim,' he rejoined brusquely, ignoring her flush of annoyance at his discourtesy.

He hoisted the boy effortlessly on his back; they set off in single file down a meandering trail, fragrant with the scent of bracken and pine needles. The sound of rushing water met them as they descended a steep slope, and Sara's face lit up at the grandeur of this wild and lonely place. A sheet of pure white foam cascaded down the smooth rocks, falling into a deep pool of icy water, that was surrounded by moss-covered stones and the fresh green fronds of ferns. A silver birch leaned delicate branches over the spray, while dark spruces loomed against the sky.

The spell was broken by the prosaic Stephen, who splashed into the stream to float his boats, but the magic lingered in Sara's face; she lowered herself on to a rock, its smooth surface warm from the sun. Patricia plumped down beside her, and said softly, 'I like it here. The waterfall looks like a bride's veil, doesn't it?'

Touched by the little girl's fantasy, Sara was about to reply when she noticed how David's features had tightened bleakly at Patricia's allusion. With true feminine intuition, she was sure he had once brought his fiancée to this enchanted spot, and that unhappy memories were plaguing him. She was conscious of a flash of pain at the thought of such a romantic rendezvous, and gave herself a mental shake. David Ramsay was nothing to her—she'd better keep that firmly in mind.

To break the constraint, she offered to keep an eye on Tim, while the others explored downstream. The man seemed glad of the chance to escape; his long-legged stride soon carried him out of sight. She and Tim sat quietly, lulled by the tumbling waters, until Tim pointed out a cheeky red squirrel scolding them from the safety of a tree limb. 'I think he's got his eye on the picnic,' the boy whispered.

'Perhaps we'd better move it, to be on the safe side,' she chuckled. 'I hear them coming back, so we can eat now anyway.'

They all tucked in with hearty appetites, and again Sara marvelled at the paradox David Ramsay presented—his lean face was relaxed and friendly when he bantered with the children, yet he treated her with distant politeness, a formality that was out of place in this wilderness retreat. After they had all eaten their fill, David carried Tim to the water's edge; the three children were soon engrossed in play. The man lit a cigarette and leaned back against a tree stump, his blue eyes remote, while Sara picked up the remains of their lunch, careful to tuck the used wrappings into the basket. Temporarily forgetting his antagonism, she joked, 'It will be much easier for me to be independent on the way up—the basket is far lighter!'

For a moment, his lips seemed about to curve in an answering smile, before he retreated behind a barrier of indifference. She gave a sharp sigh of frustration.

Mildly sarcastic, he queried, 'What's the matter, Miss Haydon? Disappointed because I don't fall at your feet, like all the other admirers a beautiful girl like you must have collected?'

She retorted resentfully, 'You make me sound the kind of female who's nothing but a man-hunter!'

'Basically, that's what all woman are.'

'Well, I'm not,' she contradicted, annoyed by his cynicism. 'I'm not the slightest bit interested in adding you to my collection, as you so elegantly put it. I did want to be friends, which is apparently an impossibility as far as you're concerned.'

He leaned forward to grasp her wrist with bruising strength. 'You're quite right,' he snapped contemptuously. 'So you can forget your feminine wiles when I'm around; it would be a shame to waste them.'

Tension crackled in the air between them, and there was a tremor in her voice when Sara spoke. 'Please, let go. You're hurting my arm.' She felt a ridiculous urge to burst into tears, and turned away, biting her lip, and holding on to the shreds of her pride. Patricia called something, the words drowned by the steady roar of the falls, and Sara stumbled down the bank to join her. Hateful man, she never wanted to see him again!

Splashing around with the children, she forced him out of her mind; for the rest of the afternoon, she resolutely avoided any direct conversation with him. On his part, if he was regretting his hasty speech, he certainly made no sign of it. When he finally dropped off the three of them at the Rutherfords', Sara heaved a deep sigh of relief, then gave a nervous start as Marilyn said behind her, 'What on earth was that for?'

'I'm afraid Mr Ramsay and I have taken a definite dislike to each other. Talk about a woman-hater!'

'Oh, dear,' Marilyn deplored. 'I know he can be very aggravating. I wish you could have met him four years ago, he was a different person. As it is, if he isn't careful, he'll turn into a crusty old bachelor.'

'I think he already has,' Sara said decisively. She met Marilyn's eyes; suddenly they both began to giggle like a couple of schoolgirls, and the blow which David's contempt had dealt her self-esteem was greatly eased.

CHAPTER THREE

LATER that evening, Stephen voiced the suggestion she had subconsciously been dreading. 'Tomorrow, let's go to Tim's house—he has an electric train set, with bridges, and signals that move and a tunnel.'

She knew, sooner or later, she would have to face David Ramsay in his own surroundings; it was ridiculous to feel nervous at the prospect. He wasn't an ogre, and he did have a charming nephew. Yet somehow he wielded a power over her that she had never experienced before: whenever she saw him, she was painfully aware of his physical proximity, of his intense masculinity; the contradictions in his personality completely baffled her. Her initial dislike had changed into an unwilling desire to penetrate his unfriendly façade. On the other hand, her common sense warned her to keep her distance, for this man could hurt her as no man had before.

So it was with a rather cowardly sense of relief that she heard rain drumming on the roof the next day, and knew the visit would have to be postponed; lightheartedly, she supervised the children's painting and modelling activities during the day. By late afternoon the weather had cleared a little.

'Why don't you take the car and go out for a while, Sara?' Marilyn proposed. 'I'll keep an eye on the children.'

'I would like to post a letter. It's only about a mile to the post office, isn't it? Perhaps I'll walk—I enjoy the exercise, especially after being in the house all day.'

'Is that how you stay so slim?' Marilyn sighed as she

regarded her plump form. 'Oh, well, Harold loves me the way I am, and dieting does take a lot of fun out of life. Have a good walk. By the way, the postmistress will probably want to know your life history, so be prepared!'

A few minutes later, Sara set out, inhaling deep breaths of the rain-washed air. The main road was bordered by tall trees, and wild flowers filled the ditches with their homely blossoms. She caught an occasional glimpse of the secluded residences of the wealthy summer visitors, down near the beach. The humbler homes of the local people dotted the road on either side. Walking by, Sara would see a net curtain move, and smiled to herself; if this was anything like the village where she and Uncle Matthew had lived, her progress was being closely followed.

The post office turned out to be an untidy cubby-hole in the back of someone's house, and a delicious smell of gingerbread, fresh from the oven, wafted in with the postmistress. She was an elderly woman with a bright smile, and the sharp eyes of a bird continually searching for crumbs. 'Can I help you, miss?' she inquired; in spite of herself, before she left, Sara had divulged her name, where she was from, and why she was staying at the Rutherfords'. 'Well then, I'll give you Mr Rutherford's letters,' the old lady said, casually extracting them from a disorderly heap on the table. 'I hope you'll enjoy your summer here.'

Still somewhat bemused, Sara stepped out into the drizzle then had to conquer a timorous impulse to retreat: David Ramsay was coming up the path towards her.

'Good afternoon, Miss Haydon. No dog with you today?'

'Good afternoon,' she replied crisply, and would have walked past him, but he moved his tall body to block her way. Her temper flared. 'Excuse me, please.'

His own expression hardened as he said bluntly, 'I think we should have a talk about Timothy. Would you wait a minute while I post this letter?'

It sounded more like an order than a request, Sara mused resentfully. She trailed through the wet grass near the road, aware that she was thereby denying the little postmistress the pleasure of overhearing any conversation that might ensue.

David Ramsay overtook her and began abruptly, 'It occurred to me after our discussion at Harold's party that possibly you were unwilling to take on the responsibility of a third child for the summer. I don't doubt your competence; presumably Harold was satisfied with that before he hired you. But after all, you were supposed to look after two children, not three. So I don't imagine you'd object if I augmented your salary?'

In blank astonishment, she stared up at the grim-featured man confronting her. 'You thought all I wanted was more money for looking after Tim?' she repeated incredulously.

'Exactly,' he shrugged. 'Why else should you do it?' His mouth thinned cynically as he continued, 'My experience of women has been that none of you do anything without recompense.'

'Mr Ramsay,' she interrupted furiously, 'I'm not interested in your experience of women. I understood from Mr Rutherford that I would be looking after Tim before he hired me, and I'm perfectly satisfied with my salary, it's more than adequate. And now, will you please excuse me. . .'

He grasped her roughly by the sleeve, but before she could protest, he demanded, 'Yes, but why should you take on Tim? He's nothing to you.'

Her anger subsided, for the strain and scepticism in his

expression roused her compassion, and it suddenly became important to her that he should understand. One part of her very conscious of his closeness, she paused a moment to sort out her thoughts, then replied as honestly as she could. 'Mr Ramsay, it's very simple. I like children; I always have. In my work, I'm used to coping with a whole ward of sick ones, and believe me, three healthy children are a pleasure after that. Tim is a dear little boy, and I'll do my best with him, as I do with Patricia and Stephen. I assure you, I'm not just motivated by money.' Her mouth quirked, giving her face a gamine charm. 'I know it's necessary, as anyone does who's been without it. But I look after children because I love doing it. And now, I really must go, or I'll be late for supper.'

The grip on her arm loosened; his eyes were puzzled as they gazed into her candid grey ones. She had the feeling he wanted to believe her, but somehow could not bring himself to do so. Wishing there was some way she could convince him, and at the same time wondering why it should matter to her, she said goodbye, and walked away into the mist, very much aware of him watching her departure. What an unfathomable man! What could have happened between him and his fiancée? Why had they parted? Whatever the reason, it had certainly left him badly scarred, with a low opinion of the female sex, she thought wryly. And once again, that night she found herself starring at the painting on the wall, as if it could explain the mystery.

The weather was still damp and foggy the following day, but by two o'clock Stephen was clearly craving some exercise. 'Can we go and see Tim now, Sara? If we walk there, Daddy said he'd pick us up at supper time.'

She couldn't resist his coaxing, so, resigned to the inevitable, she pulled on rubber boots and put on a raincoat over her jeans. They trudged down the beach, gulls mewing mournfully overhead, while waves lapped lazily at the rocks. Despite her resolutions, Sara became increasingly apprehensive as they wound up the path through the woods and came in sight of David Ramsay's summer home. Built of lightly stained cedar, and great sheets of plate glass, it was clearly no mass-produced dwelling, but an architect's masterpiece. Its angled roof was shaded by tall pines, and smoke rose lazily from the huge, breachstone chimney. Situated on a slight rise overlooking the ocean, it blended perfectly into its wild surroundings. Sara was completely taken aback, for the house exuded an aura of money, money spent lovingly, with considerable attention to detail. She thought of David's ancient jeep and well-worn clothes – yet another paradox in this contradictory man.

Stephen rang the bell, and it was David who opened the door, the genuine welcome in his expression lightening Sara's spirits. 'I'm glad to see you,' he admitted. 'Timothy's been cooped up all morning, and badly needs company.'

Slightly deflated that he apparently was pleased to see them only for Tim's sake, Sara knelt to undo the clasps on Patricia's raincoat, her fingers fumbling nervously. She rose, and he helped her off with her own coat, his hands brushing her shoulders. 'Come in by the fire, Miss Haydon. Or should we dispense with formality, and be Sara and David?'

There was a quizzical, almost taunting lift to his brows, and she was suddenly tired of all this verbal fencing. Her chin lifted defiantly. 'I am already called Sara by your nephew, and I certainly don't intend to call you Uncle David, so I think you have the right idea.'

The coldness faded from his gaze as they confronted each other in the narrow hall. Spontaneously, his mouth widened in an appreciative grin. 'Truce,' he said, and shook her hand firmly. 'Now come and warm yourself, it's chilly walking on a day like this, your fingers are like ice.'

She was quite unprepared for the mellow beauty of the room they entered; she paused on the threshold, David close behind her, while her fascinated gaze explored it. The polished hardwood floor was covered by an Oriental rug, intricately patterned in deep reds and blues. Heavy blue curtains flanked the picture windows, and outlined the view of mist, trees and distant shore. The furniture was Danish modern; gracefully shaped Dutch pewter and Swedish glass decorated the mantel of the stone fireplace, in which flames leaped cheerfully.

'You must have been to Scandinavia,' Sara said, delighted by the twinkle in her companion's eye as he responded.

'Yes, I spent a summer there two years ago, and rather fell for their designs, as you can see!'

A teak cabinet was taken up by Eskimo sculpture, and Sara picked up a miniature caribou, its stone surface satin-smooth, its ivory antlers delicately carved from walrus tusks. 'I've done quite a bit of travelling in the north, too, collecting the legends and mythology of the Eskimos,' David remarked. 'I hope eventually to teach a course in it. They're a very friendly and hospitable people, but I'm afraid their way of life is increasingly threatened by the white man's idea of progress. An old man in Inuvik gave me that carving.'

Built-in teak bookshelves, that lined the entire opposite wall, drew Sara's attention; her hands ran over the books as though greeting old friends. She swung round to face David, her grey eyes warm with remembrance. 'My father had a bookshop in England. It wasn't very big, particularly by American standards, but we loved it.

I used to help him unpack the new books, and arrange them on the shelves. To this day, I can't resist entering a bookshop.' Heedless of her host's presence, she picked out a few old favourites, and riffled through their pages reminiscently. A much used volume of poetry caught her eye; reading the familiar verses, she was almost able to feel her father beside her.

A log crashed in the hearth. With a start, she returned to the present. It was David standing beside her instead, his blue eyes intent upon her rapt face. 'You were a long way away,' he said gently.

Whether it was the unaccustomed sympathy in his voice, or the echo of her father's beloved poetry in her ears, she heard herself telling him softly, 'Yes, two thousand miles and eleven years: he died when I was twelve. In the evenings, when the shop was closed and I'd done my homework, he'd read to me—poetry, plays, novels, a lot of it over my head, I suppose. He had a beautiful speaking voice, and I've loved books ever since. These poems have often helped me through rough spots.' She looked up at the man so quietly watching her, adding wonderingly, 'I don't know why I'm telling you this. I haven't mentioned it to anyone for years.'

What a strange effect he had on her. . .in their short acquaintance, his arrogance and cynicism had made her lose her temper, his bitterness had roused her compassion, and now his sensitivity to her mood had caused her to speak unthinkingly from her heart of experiences very dear to her. A flush stole across her cheeks. To cover her sudden confusion, she hastily changed the subject. 'I wonder what the children are up to—they seem terribly quiet.'

He tactfully followed her lead. 'Come and see the famous train. I thought I'd have to study engineering to put it together! And I'll make you a cup of tea.'

He led her down the hall to Timothy's room, where an excited Patricia ran to meet them. 'I made the signal go and smoke came out of the engine!'

Sara listened to the two boys' somewhat confused explanation of the workings of the train set, and duly admired it in action. Then, with interest, she surveyed Tim's bright and airy room, with models, books and games neatly arranged on the shelves. Quite a contrast to Stephen's haphazard untidiness! She noticed binoculars hanging beside a tidy pile of bird books on the windowsill. 'Are you a birdwatcher too, Tim?' she asked.

He swung over to her on his crutches, his small face alight with enthusiasm as he showed her the mesh bags of nesting materials, suspended outside from a tree limb. 'There are feathers and bits of wool and horsehair,' he explained. 'Blue jays and chickadees are all I've seen so far, but we have swallows nesting under the eaves of the garage; they make nests out of mud.'

'You'll have to help me out on the forest birds. My uncle always fed the birds, but we lived on an exposed coast, so all we got were seagulls and shorebirds.'

'Where does he live now?' the little boy queried.

Her face clouded. 'He died this spring, Tim.'

He nodded in grave understanding. 'You must miss him.'

She gave him a quick hug, moved by his insight. 'Yes, I do. Look, there's a bird now. What is it?'

'It's a chickadee, they nest in the spruces.'

She reached for the binoculars, and remarked, 'Once your cast is off we could go birdwatching in the woods—I'd like to do that.'

David's voice spoke from the doorway. 'Tea's ready, Sara. Cocoa and toast for the children.'

They gathered cosily around the fire, drinking out of mugs and eating quantities of hot buttered toast. Sara licked her fingers with a sigh of satisfaction. 'I've been eating like a horse since I came here, it must be the sea air. If I get fat, I'll blame it on that anyway!'

David laughed, speculatively eyeing her slender figure. 'I don't think you have to worry. Still, I always find food tastes better here too.'

The children wandered back to the playroom, and the two of them chatted lazily together in front of the dying fire, amicably bickering over their favourite authors. The peace and comfort of the room enfolded the girl in a cloak of contentment. For the first time since their turbulent initial meeting, she found herself thinking what a wonderful friend this man would make, for he was revealing a gentleness and depth to his nature, that she had not foreseen.

He reached into the woodbox for a new log, and, as he straightened, winced sharply with sudden pain. Seeing Sara's concerned eyes on him, he explained ruefully, 'I bruised a couple of ribs in the car accident, when Tim broke his leg. Every now and then they remind me.'

'I must have hurt you the other day, when I bumped into you,' she said tentatively.

'Oh, it was nothing. The trouble was, I'd been up most of the night before with Tim; he still has nightmares about the accident—his parents were killed that way, and maybe he associates the two accidents, I don't know. Anyway, I was peacefully asleep in the sun, when in rapid succession the dog ran over me and you ran into me.' He paused, and awkwardly concluded, 'I shouldn't have bitten your head off, though. I'm sorry.'

She smiled her acceptance of his apology. They heard a crunch of tyres on the gravel, and David got up, stretching out his hand to help her to her feet. 'That must be Harold, he's early.'

Driving home a little later, Sara was pervaded by a

glow of well-being, after the unexpectedly pleasant afternoon. To think that she had dreaded it! Her fingers tingled from the remembered warmth of David's clasp, and she found herself wondering if she would see him tomorrow. . .

However, during the next few days she met him only casually, while taking Timothy home, or picking him up in the mornings. Because the weather had warmed appreciably, the Rutherfords were golfing every day, and she was kept busy with the children and their pursuits. It was inevitable that, at times, Tim was unable to accompany them; he could not paddle in the sea, or even walk on the beach without his crutches sinking on the soft sand. Sara could see the envy in his face during Stephen's description of their hike around Twin Island Lake, and she said comfortingly, 'It's not much longer until your cast comes off, is it, Tim?'

He sighed. 'It seems like ages. It itches in the hot weather.'

So, as much as possible, Sara planned outings that could include him. One sunny afternoon, when his uncle was away, she drove them all into the picnic grounds at the lake. While Patricia and Stephen splashed in the shallow water, she and Timothy sat watching for birds; their patience was rewarded when a pair of tiny yellow and black warblers flew into the maple above them, and flitted among the leafy branches. They cooked hot dogs over a fire, then toasted marshmallows in the coals, feeding the scraps to the brazen red squirrels. And when Sara drove Tim home, later that evening, she was pleased to see he was as grubby as a normal boy, with colour in his cheeks and a suntan on his arms.

That night a sudden Atlantic storm swept up the coast, bringing sheets of rain, which pelted against the windowpanes. The soaked tree limbs thrashed against each other in the gale; the breakers roared with a deep, continuous thunder.

At breakfast, Marilyn remarked with disappointment, 'No golf today. The trouble is, the course will still be wet tomorrow. Perhaps we'll take the children to visit the Campbells, they wanted us to go one day this week. I'll see what Harold thinks.'

Sara produced large sheets of newspaper and poster paint, so the two children happily and messily painted all morning. Marilyn explained, as they ate lunch, that the Campbells had invited them for dinner. 'I feel a bit guilty leaving you alone on such a dreadful day, particularly as Mrs Donnelly will be out visiting too. Do you mind?'

'Not at all,' Sara assured her. 'I have a new library book—I'll curl up by the fire and be thoroughly lazy.' After they left, she amused herself making Miss Moppet a pair of slacks and a matching top, as a surprise for Patricia, but for some reason her book failed to hold her attention.

Restless and unsettled, she gazed out of the window; the rain had abated, although the wind still whipped the trees. I'll take Ben up the beach to the Point, she thought, the surf should be beautiful there. In hooded anorak and boots, she left the house, pushing against the gale with her head down, the cold rain stinging her face. The storm's intensity was almost frightening; too stubborn to retreat, she was gasping for breath when she finally reached the partial shelter of the stunted spruces on the Point. The wild tumult of the sea made the effort worthwhile. Great waves heaved upwards and smashed against the rocks, spray hurling itself high in the air. She licked her lips, tasting the salt on them. The ceaseless roar of the frenzied ocean battered her ears; the wind tugged at her sodden coat and pushed her back against the tree trunk.

She heard Benedict's deep bark, and turned to call him, the words dying on her lips as she saw David Ramsay's tall figure striding up the slope towards her. In an old ski jacket, his wet hair dishevelled, he looked very much a part of the wildness of the storm. He shouted above the waves' clamour, 'A fellow lunatic! Don't you know all sensible people are home huddled around their fireplaces?'

Sara laughed, brushing at the raindrops that trickled down her cheeks. 'Isn't it marvellous! I just couldn't stay indoors.'

For several minutes, the majesty of the scene held them spellbound. Then a capricious gust buffeted Sara's slight body, and as she staggered unsteadily, his strong arm came around her shoulders. 'Hold on, I wouldn't want to lose you over the cliff.'

Feeling very secure in the circle of his arm, she smiled at him shyly. His blue eyes looked deep into hers; his head bent, and their lips met in a strangely gentle kiss that, nevertheless, stirred her to the depths of her being. As they drew slowly apart, a wayward curtain of spray blew against them, and he pulled her hard against his jacket for shelter. To make himself heard, he put his mouth close to her ear. 'Can you come back with me for a while, or are the Rutherfords waiting for you?'

'I'm on my own today, I'd love to come,' she shouted back.

He grabbed her hand and they raced down the slope like two children, Benedict loping along behind. 'I'll race you home,' Sara challenged mischievously.

They dashed up the dunes, the wind behind them, and reached the house panting and spent.

'A tie!' proclaimed David, when they collapsed laughing in the hallway. 'You know, Timothy told me you were fun to be with, I have to agree with him. He's watching television next door with a friend. Let me take your coat, Sara. The bathroom's at the end of the hall, if you want to dry yourself off a bit. I'll start the fire. How would you like a hot buttered rum?'

'Mmm, sounds wonderful.' She gazed at her radiant face in the bathroom mirror. He kissed me, she thought. I felt so safe, and yet so alive, in his arms. I've never met anyone like him before.

A tendril of hair straggled across her face, and she abruptly descended to practicalities. Heavens, look at my hair, it's soaking. What a mess! Trying to smooth it down with her fingers, she made her way to the kitchen. It was a neat and workmanlike room, equipped with electrical appliances galore. 'You don't have a hairbursh I could use, do you, David?'

'Sure, just a minute.'

When he returned, she asked with interest, 'Do you do all your own cooking?'

'Usually, yes. Tim helps wash up afterwards. Mind you, we don't have anything very elaborate. I have a cleaning lady twice a week, to get rid of the worst of the dust.' He grinned at her. 'Here's your brush. Do you want to check the fire for me, while I mix the drinks?'

She went through to the living room, again impressed by its skilful blend of style and comfort. A tiny painting over the stereo caught her eye—surely it was a Chardin still life, its jewel-like hues as perfect as the day it was painted. He noticed her interest.

'Gorgeous thing, isn't it? Makes my own efforts look a bit sick.'

'Oh, I don't know about that,' she said thoughtlessly. 'I like your painting of the chrysanthemums.'

'Of course, that's at Harold's, isn't it? Whereabouts have they put it?'

Embarrassed, she wished she'd never started the

conversation. 'It's in my bedroom. I think it's beautiful,' she said staunchly, very much aware of his quizzical eyes on her pink cheeks.

'Thank you for your kind words. At least it's not giving you nightmares! I must get my oils out again, it's a long time since I've touched them.'

He unplugged the kettle, and she fled back to the fire, pushing Benedict out of the way so she could kneel on the rug. As the warmth of the flames spread, she began to brush her heavy, dark hair.

David sat down on the floor, his back against the armchair, and passed her a steaming, fragrant mug. Half serious and half amused, he commented, 'You're a rare woman, Sara. After that wind and rain, I would think most females would require a lot more than a hairbrush to repair the damage.' His voice deepened. 'You're beautiful as you are; I like a girl to look natural.'

She blushed with pleasure, and he teased, 'Look, now—no blusher on the market could beat that!' Sobering, he requested, 'Tell me about yourself, Sara. Harold mentioned you were a physiotherapist in Montreal—what made you leave?'

She hesitated, the unhappy memories of those last weeks in the city flooding back. 'You remember I told you my father died when I was twelve. My only other relative was his elder brother in Nova Scotia, so I came to Canada to live with him; he died this spring. It was a great shock to me, and somehow I just couldn't settle back into my job, and the routine of life in Montreal—I couldn't stand the crowds and the perpetual noise. Uncle Matthew's house was built on the cliffs, overlooking the ocean, so you can see why I'm so happy here; and the Rutherfords are very good to me. I doubt if I'll go back to Montreal, I don't seem to be a big city person.'

He nodded sympathetically. 'I know what you mean.

Tim and I live on the outskirts of Rochford; after ten minutes' driving, you can leave the houses behind, and there's nothing but wilderness for miles. That's the beauty of this country—room to breathe, so much of it empty and waiting to be explored. Then we come up here quite a bit. It's beautiful in the winter under a deep snow, the bay packed with drift ice. I'm lucky enough to have the best of both worlds: I enjoy my work—I teach English at the university in Rochford—and my summers are free to come to the Cape, although I try to keep my hand in with a bit of writing. I spent the morning on an article for a literary journal—hence the need for fresh air this afternoon!'

They smiled at each other, in perfect accord, happiness highlighting Sara's face. 'I'm starting to feel hungry,' David admitted. 'How would an omelette taste?'

'You just want to show off your prowess in the kitchen! Let me help.'

'If it's a failure, I shall blame you,' he retorted, a wicked glint in his eye. 'You're quite a distraction, you know.'

They ate by the fire, the omelettes melting in their mouths. In the background, piano music rippled from the stereo, and outside dusk fell. Afterwards they washed up together, talking companionably over the domestic task. Reaching over to hang the cloth on the rack, Sara dropped it accidentally; they simultaneously bent to pick it up, her head bumped his chin, and his arm came around her waist to steady her.

'Sorry, Sara, did I hurt you? That's what comes of trying to be chivalrous!' He helped her to her feet, his hands warm on her bare arms. 'Sure you're all right?'

She nodded, feeling her heart flutter at his nearness. He went on slowly, 'I've never met a girl like you before:

honest and straightforward, and yet so feminine. You're making me forget I'm supposed to be a staid and dignified professor.' He grimaced in annoyance as the phone rang suddenly, and left the room to answer it.

Sara didn't know whether to be glad of the interruption or not. She knew the man stirred her, rousing feelings that she had not known existed. In some strange way, she could both tease him, and yet tell him her deepest emotions. But she had only known him such a short time. . .and their acquaintance had hardly had an auspicious beginning.

He rejoined her in the kitchen; his mood had changed, for he said casually, 'Why don't you borrow that volume of poems you were looking at the other day? I meant to give it to you then, but it slipped my mind.'

'Thank you, I'd like to. I'll take good care of it.' Just as she selected the book, her elbow knocked a novel from the lower shelf. A coloured photograph fell from between its pages. She retrieved it, and saw a strikingly attractive blonde, her head resting on David's shoulder, their arms entwined. With a quick pang, she knew it must be Linda, the fiancée Marilyn had mentioned. She was about to replace the picture in the book, when David's body loomed over her, and he snatched it from her fingers. She was horrified by the harsh lines of bitterness on his face as he stared at the laughing couple. With a violent gesture, his fist crumpled the photograph, and he flung it in the fire.

Sara felt a sharp pain clench her heart; he must still love this Linda, to be affected so strongly by a mere photograph. He turned back to her, his eyes forbidding and cold, his voice distant. 'That was Timothy on the phone, asking me to get him. I'll take you home on the way.'

Distressed and frightened by the change in him, she

pulled on her coat and boots, and called the dog; David drove her to the Rutherfords' in complete silence, his gaze grimly concentrated on the wet road. As he pulled up by the dark and empty house, he looked at her, his features tense and pale in the dim light, and a wave of pity swept over her. 'David,' she faltered, 'what's wrong?'

He seemed about to speak, but then his mouth tightened, and his eyes shut her out. 'Nothing. Goodnight.'

She let herself out of the car and ran up the steps, thankful there was no one to see the tears on her lashes. In her room, the glowing colours of David's painting swam before her eyes; so that long-ago love was not dead. Yet surely he had been moved by genuine emotion when he had kissed her in the rain! Where had the gentle strength of that David gone? She experienced a desolate sense of loss that frightened her—how could she feel this way, when she scarcely knew him?

For a long time that night she lay and stared into the darkness. In the morning, she was tired and heavy-eyed, and when Stephen suggested a walk to the Point, her refusal was unwontedly sharp. The boy looked so disconcerted by her irritability that she said contritely, 'Oh, Stephen, I'm sorry, I'm out of sorts today.'

Timothy commented, 'Uncle David is cross today too. He said he didn't sleep well.'

Hurriedly, she proposed, 'Why don't we go to Trout Brook in the car? We could play on the swings and seesaws there.' This suggestion met with approval; and when they reached the playground, Sara was kept busy enough pushing swings, and helping Tim keep his balance, that her unhappy thoughts were relegated to the back of her mind.

CHAPTER FOUR

EARLY the following afternoon, the phone rang; Sara picked it up and a small voice said, 'Sara? It's Tim. Uncle David's not feeling well. Could you come and get me, and then I'd be out of his way?'

She warmed to the appeal in his tone. 'Of course, I'll be there in five minutes.'

When she arrived, there was no sign of David, but Tim was waiting patiently in the driveway, leaning on his crutches. He looked so pleased to see her that she gave him a quick hug as she helped him into the car. Trying to sound casual, she asked, 'What's wrong with your uncle, Tim?'

'He's got an awful headache. He gets them every now and then since the accident. The doctor said they'd go away soon, and he has yellow pills to take; but the pills make him really sleepy, so that's why I asked you to take me,' he finished breathlessly.

It was late that evening when the two of them returned, and the house was quiet and dark, without any signs of life. A bit worried, Sara suggested, 'Perhaps I'd better come in with you, while you get ready for bed, Tim.'

'Ok,' he readily agreed, transparently relieved by her words.

They crept quietly in the back door, and Sara slipped off her shoes before following Tim to his room. David's door was ajar; she stood there silently for a minute, until reassured by the rhythm of heavy breathing from within. She tucked Tim into bed, giving him a glass of milk and a biscuit, then read to him quietly until his eyelids began to droop. As she leaned over to kiss him goodnight, he murmured, 'I wish you could be my mother, Sara. I miss not having one.'

'I know. I don't remember mine. Everyone else at school except me had a mother to go to concerts and visiting days. But I loved my father very much, just as you love your uncle and that makes up for a lot.'

Quite unselfconsciously, he put his arms around her neck and sleepily kissed her, then snuggled under the blankets. A rush of protective love filled her; she switched out his bedside lamp, saying softly, 'Goodnight, Tim dear. Sleep well, and I'll see you tomorrow.'

Something moved in the dark shadows of the hallway; she suppressed a shriek of alarm as a black figure moved towards her. 'Oh, David,' she whispered, 'you frightened me. I thought you were asleep.'

In the dim light she stared up at him, shocked by his pale and haggard appearance. Leaning against the wall for support, and rubbing at his forehead, he focussed his eyes on her with difficulty. 'Those pills really knock me out. Did you only just bring Tim home?'

'Yes, I kept him until bedtime.' She hesitated, still uncertain of her reception. 'Let me make you a cup of tea, David. Would you like something to eat?'

'Why do you bother with me, Sara?' he groaned. 'I was so damn rude to you the other day.'

'Yes, you were rather,' she said honestly. 'But that was the other day, and I don't like holding grudges.' Calmly she persisted, 'Are you hungry?'

He considered, fingering the rough stubble on his chin. 'Well, I could do with something. I haven't eaten since last night. I'll go and clean up a bit first.'

Sara busied herself in the kitchen, filled with contentment that he had lowered his defences enough to let her help him. When he returned, he had changed from his rumpled trousers and shirt into pyjamas and a silk dressing-gown, and his face was clean-shaven. She sat at the table with him while he ate the light meal she had prepared; after he had finished, he lit a cigarette and sat back.

'That feels better. Thank you, Sara. I'd better stay up for a while now, or I won't be able to sleep tonight. I hate to take too many of those pills—I'm always afraid I won't hear Tim if he wakes. He's fairly highly strung under that quiet exterior of his, and I think I told you he's been having nightmares since the car accident.'

She started to tidy up the kitchen, feeling very much at home in her role of helpmeet; his husky voice broke into her tranquil thoughts.

'You mentioned at the post office that day that you had once been without money. What did you mean?'

Surprised at his interest, but willing to humour him, Sara paused in recollection. 'Money was never in great supply at any time in my life. I don't think my father was much of a business man. He'd almost give books away to hard-up students who needed them, and he loved to see the children of the neighbourhood coming with their pennies, to buy books that usually cost a lot more. When he died, what was left after the sale of the shop covered his debts and the funeral expenses; Uncle Matthew sent me the money for my passage to Canada.'

She shivered suddenly, remembering the bleak misery of the ocean voyage. She had been desperately lonely for her father, and each day of the crossing had increased the distance from everything that was familiar, and taken her nearer to an unknown country and an unknown relative. . .

'It was a dreadful journey,' she continued in a low voice. 'Everyone was so kind, and all I wanted was to be left alone. And how I hated my first few weeks in Canada! It was early April – spring in England – the fields were knee-deep in snow, the lakes frozen, ice cold winds blowing off the sea. There never was a spring as I knew it, the trees didn't even come into leaf until the end of May. I suppose I'd pulled up so many roots when I crossed the Atlantic, I'd have been miserable wherever I went. Fortunately, Uncle Matthew was very understanding, and let me take my time. It wasn't really too long before I came to love my new uncle and my new surroundings.

'He had arthritis quite badly—consequently he depended mainly on his pension; I found out afterwards, he'd used up most of his savings to bring me to Canada. So when I went away to study therapy, it was a hard struggle financially. I worked in the summers and had part-time jobs in the winter too. Luckily the two old ladies next door to Uncle Matthew had taught me to sew, so at least my clothes didn't cost much. When I started working in Montreal, I always sent him any extra money I had; I was telling Tim how he loved to watch the seabirds on the cliffs, and he was finally able to buy a pair of expensive binoculars he'd coveted for years. He only used them a few months.'

She broke off, very near tears. 'You must be a good listener, David. I always seem to be telling you things I've never told anyone else. I didn't intend to burden you with such a monologue!' Feeling on dangerous ground, she fell silent, concentrating instead on rinsing the sink and putting the plates away.

He teased gently, 'I enjoy your monologues, as you call them. I'm going to sit down for a while—come and keep me company, hmm?'

'As soon as I've finished,' she promised. He went in to sit by the fire; when she rejoined him, his eyes were closed, his head resting against the back of the chair, lines of pain scoring his face.

She peeped in at Tim, who lay completely relaxed in sleep. Switching on the light in David's room, she made his bed with professional skill, although for a moment her fingers lingered on the indentation his head had made in the pillow. She walked back down the hallway, her bare feet soundless on the thick carpet, and David said drowsily, 'Can you stay a bit longer? I'm afraid I'm not very bright company, though.'

'I don't mind, I'm quite happy just to sit and relax. Patricia and Stephen were in bed when I left, and Marilyn knows where I am if she needs me.'

She fetched a book from the shelves, and subsided on to the rug with slender grace, propping her back against the chair, her face serene in the dancing firelight as she began to read. To anyone looking in from outside, it would have seemed a peaceful and domestic scene, until with a muffled groan, David leaned forward, resting his head on his hands.

Sara glanced up in concern. 'Is it worse, David?'

'I feel as though there's a sledgehammer pounding away inside my head,' he muttered.

She got up, unable to sit still while he was in pain. 'I think you'd better go back to bed, let me help you.' She staggered under his weight as he got unsteadily to his feet.

'I can't even see straight, Sara.'

'Perhaps I should call the doctor.'

'There's no point. I was told to expect this kind of thing, it's an after-effect of the concussion. I'll be Ok.'

She accompanied him to his room, took his dressing gown and hung it up, desperately worried by his deathly pale face and tightly clenched jaw. She couldn't leave him like this. . . in sudden decision, she said briskly,

'Lie down, David, and I'll rub your back for you, that can ease a migraine.'

Too miserable to argue, or to assert his male independence, he did as he was told; she sat on the bed beside him, her supple fingers slowly kneading his neck and shoulders, working the tension out of the taut muscles. He was naked to the waist, and for the first time in her career as a therapist, she was tinglingly aware of the physical magnetism of the body beneath her hands. It was difficult to be businesslike, for her treacherous hands longed to caress the strong column of his neck. Stop it, Sara, she mentally chided herself. Behave yourself!

To her infinite relief, the lines on his face eventually smoothed, and his body relaxed. Unsure whether or not he was asleep, she shifted her cramped knees, abruptly aware of the lateness of the hour, the utterly silent house, and the misinterpretations that could be placed upon her presence in David's bedroom at this time of night. She said softly, 'I must go. Will you be all right now?'

He raised himself on one elbow, and detained her with his hand on her wrist, his blue eyes vulnerable and deeply serious. 'Thank you, Sara, from Tim and especially from me. I don't know how I'd have managed today without you. Drive carefully, my dear.' He pulled her down to him, and his lips brushed hers in a kiss whose sweetness turned her bones to water. 'Goodnight,' he said huskily.

It was an effort for her to reply calmly, 'I'll get Tim early tomorrow, so you won't have to look after him.'

She let herself out of the house, and drove back to the Rutherfords', firmly keeping her mind on the road. Once there, she stood by the car and gazed up at the distant stars, mulling over the puzzle of David's personality. In the cold light of morning, would he resent her for having seen him with his guard down, his weakness exposed?

And what had he meant by that parting endearment? She didn't think he was the type of man to use them lightly. . . Her reverie was interrupted by Harold, who called from the veranda, 'Sara? How's David?'

'He's really miserable,' she confessed. 'I wanted to call the doctor, but he wouldn't let me. I told him I'd keep Tim tomorrow, though.'

'The doctors claim he'll get over these headaches. We've been watching the late movie on television. Join us, and I'll make you a drink. You've had a long day.'

Sara didn't see David the next morning, because Tim was waiting for her outside, but at lunchtime Harold reported he was on his feet again. She made a quick trip to the post office later in the afternoon; while looking through the letters, she was hailed by Dr Callaghan's bluff voice. 'Sara, how nice to see you again! You're looking very pretty today. If I were twenty years younger, I'd give the fellows around here a run for their money.'

'You're full of blarney! Do you talk to your patients like that?'

'Of course, part of the cure. Seriously, I've been meaning to get in touch with you. You've been keeping an eye on Tim Ramsey, haven't you, as well as the Rutherford children? His cast is due to come off in two or three days, so he'll need therapy. How would you like to take him on? We're badly understaffed at the hospital, and he'd probably have to go into Saraguay, otherwise. I mentioned the possibility to Harold, and he was quite amenable.'

Sara hesitated. 'What about Tim's uncle? Is it all right with him?'

'I'll be talking to him later today, to set up the appointment for Tim, but I wanted to check with you first. He should be glad to get someone as highly qualified as you.'

'More flattery, Dr Callaghan,' she laughed. 'Yes, I'd be happy to do it. I've been feeling rather guilty about my lazy summer—this will keep me in practice.'

'Fine. I'll let you know when the appointment is, so you can come in with them, and I can show you what I want done. Well, I'd better get back to my house calls. Thanks, Sara.' He waved and roared off in a bright red sports car, that matched his ebullient personality.

Idly jingling the car keys, the girl pondered the implications of the doctor's request. So Tim was finally getting rid of his unwieldy cast. She vowed to do her best to have him running and swimming with the other children, as soon as he possibly could. Clearly, she would be seeing quite a bit more of David in the near future. . . The prospect was a pleasant one, and she ignored the tiny voice of caution from her subconscious, that warned her to beware of this man, for just as he awakened emotions she had never felt before, so could he hurt her as she had never been hurt before. Nonsense, she thought. I like him, and want to understand him better, that's all.

She drove home. After giving Harold his letters, she and the children weeded the vegetable garden in the warm sun. They ambled back to the house, where, with a jolt, Sara recognised the car parked in the shade as David's. Conscious of her untidy hair and muddy hands, she went around to the back door, hoping to reach her room unobserved. But luck was against her—David was standing in the kitchen, chatting to Harold. For a moment, amused admiration shone in his blue eyes. Wisps of hair fell over her heat-flushed face, and her bare arms and legs were already smoothly tanned.

'Hold on a minute,' he said, reaching for a cloth by the sink and wetting it under the tap. He walked towards her, while she waited in mingled alarm and exasperation—what on earth was he going to do?

Deliberately, he tilted her chin up with one hand, and with the other, wiped away a long smear of mud on her cheek, showing her the dirt on the cloth. His eyes glinting with mischief, he said gravely, 'There, that's better. I said I liked you to look natural, but I didn't mean you had to bring half the garden in with you.'

She blushed, very aware of Harold's appreciation of this little scene. 'Men!' she exclaimed indignantly. 'I shall go and make myself presentable for dinner, if you'll both excuse me. At least I won't have to bother washing my face!'

Sara, in the meantime, was wondering if she would ever be able to anticipate what David would do next. She was warmed by a glow of excitement while she showered, then dressed carefully in a crisply tailored pale yellow shirtwaist, twisting her dark hair up on her head. In defiance of David and his 'natural' look, she applied eye-shadow and a touch of mascara, that emphasised the beauty of her deep grey eyes and long lashes. After all, she justified herself, Marilyn always dressed for dinner. Consequently, when they sat down around the gleaming table, she had the poise she needed to hide the inner turmoil David's presence caused.

'I was talking to Dr Callaghan,' he remarked, as they sipped coffee and liqueurs. 'The appointment is on Friday, could I pick you up around two?'

'Yes, that would be fine.' She smiled at Tim. 'Are you counting the hours? You're to have your own personal physiotherapist, you know.'

'I can personally recommend her, too,' David intervened incorrigibly, grinning when the girl glared at him. 'If I may be serious, though, Sara, I never really thanked you for your help last night. I slept like a log after you left, and I'm back to normal today. She'll have you running around in no time, Tim.'

'That'll be great,' the little boy enthused, cheerfully oblivious of Sara's pink cheeks.

'We have cause for celebration, as well,' Harold added, amused at this byplay. 'We had a letter today from my younger brother Charles; he's coming to stay with us for two or three weeks. You wouldn't have met him, David. He's been the European representative for his firm for the past six years, and this will be his first visit here—typical of Charles after not seeing us for two years, to let us know on Wednesday he's coming on Sunday. We'll have to have a party for him next week, Marilyn, maybe a barbecue if the good weather will hold.'

He stopped in sudden consternation. 'Hey, that reminds me—there were two letters for you yesterday, Sara. I must have left them in my jacket pocket.' He left the table, and returned holding them in his hand. 'I'm sorry, I'm not usually that forgetful. I guess Charles's news put it out of my mind.'

'You're forgiven,' she said lightly. 'One's from Joan, a friend in Montreal, and this one's from your sister. Maybe she has news of a job, she said she'd let me know if she heard of any. Would you excuse me a minute, please?' She moved to the lamp shining by the window, straining to read Miss Rutherford's rather illegible handwriting.

My dear Sara,

Thank you for your letter, I was so glad to hear everything is going well, and that you are happy with Marilyn and Harold. Admittedly I'm prejudiced, but I'm very fond of my brother and his wife. And as you say, it's really a beautiful place.

I'm sending you the two latest physiotherapy journals, there are several advertisements you might be interested in. But perhaps you'll end up with Dr

Callaghan? Dr Moore, one of our surgeons, was a classmate of his at medical school, and speaks very highly of him.

You will be pleased to hear that Deborah Kaye, on Ward Four, was discharged last week. She was much improved, her parents were delighted to see her up and around again.

'I'm sure you were sorry about Joan Madison's fiancé. I know she's a close friend of yours, and will have been in touch with you. Fortunately, the doctors are quite hopeful now; at first, it didn't look good at all. . .

What could have happened to Simon? Sara bit her lip in apprehension as she tore open Joan's letter, dreading to read its contents.

Dear Sara,

I was planning to phone you, but decided I'd probably dissolve into floods of tears, hence the letter. Simon was a passenger in the jet that crashed near Toronto last week—he'd been on a business trip to his company's head office. He's going to live—there were two days when even that was touch and go—and he'll eventually walk again. But he has a long hard road ahead of him; he'll be flat on his back in a cast for three months, and may have to have an operation. I was terrified that he'd be paralysed, but the doctors assure me there's no danger of that. You know Simon—he lives for skiing and tennis. Of course, we've had to delay the wedding, but this is the least of my worries. I don't mind waiting, if only he'll be all right.

Please write, Sara. I've wanted you here more than

once, these last few days. Hope all is well with you.
Love,
Joan.

The words blurred in front of Sara's eyes; a tiny sound of distress escaped her lips. Poor Simon. . .she was dimly conscious of a strong arm around her shoulders, and she raised her head, two tears trickling down her cheeks.

David's voice was rough with concern. 'What's wrong, my dear?'

'My best friend's fiancé has been badly hurt in that jet crash. I was very close to both of them, they were so good to me while I was in Montreal. They've had to postpone their wedding, he'll be in hospital four or five months, I would think. He won the men's slalom ski championship in Quebec two years ago.' Her tears threatened to overflow again, and David pulled out a clean handkerchief to wipe her wet cheeks.

'I'll get your sweater, and we'll go for a walk on the beach. The others will excuse us.' He kept his arm warm about her shoulders, as they left the room.

Outside, David put Sara's cardigan over her shoulders, and tucked her arm into his as they stumbled down the uneven path to the shore. 'Careful, don't trip. What actually happened to this chap, Sara? You didn't tell me his name.'

She related all she knew, her words ragged with strain. '. . . You'd like Simon, he's a fantastic skier, and plays a terrific game of tennis as well. Oh, David, he's got to get better. He and Joan are so in love, they shine with happiness when they're together. They both took me under their wing in Montreal—when you come from a country village, and are as naïve and innocent as I was, you really appreciate that kind of thing.' She sighed. 'It was quite a shock; I'll have to write to Joan tonight.'

They ambled along the soft sand, the soothing

murmur of the waves accompanying them. In need of consolation, Sara asked. 'Why do these things happen, David? It seems so cruel and unnecessary.'

He drew her closer to the warmth of his body, cradling her hand in his. 'I don't know, Sara. I doubt if anyone does. I went through a bad time myself three years ago, when James and his wife were killed, and Tim was left an orphan. James was only a year and a half younger than I, and we were always close—there were just the two of us in the family. His wife, Ginny, was a lovely girl. Their lives were snuffed out seemingly without any purpose, and for a while everything was meaningless to me. I did a lot of thinking: I guess we have to accept that these things happen, and do our best to help in any way we can, when they do. Not a very earth-shaking conclusion, I'm afraid,' he finished ruefully. 'You look tired, love, but we're nearly home. Are you feeling any better?'

'Yes, I am. Thank you for being so understanding.'

They reached the house, and his arm tightened around her. He leaned over and kissed her softly on the mouth. 'I won't come in. Sleep well, and I'll see you tomorrow.'

In the quiet of her room, Sara slowly undressed, her limbs aching with tiredness, but her tranquillity restored. How well David had recognised her feelings, and how comforting it had been to share her anxiety and doubts with him. As she drifted into a deep and dreamless sleep, she knew Joan and Simon would like him. . .a tiny smile curved the lips that he had kissed.

CHAPTER FIVE

SARA was dressed and ready when David came for her on Friday afternoon. Tim was obviously both excited and a bit apprehensive, sitting near her for reassurance. A constraint fell over the two adults, so Sara was glad of Tim's chatter as they drove along the coast, with its ever-changing pattern of rocks and surf, seabirds and wind-stunted trees.

The hospital was small, but immaculately clean; Sara looked about her with interest while they waited for Dr Callaghan. 'This way, please,' said a crisply starched nurse, who led them to a waiting room, where a receptionist entered a few minutes later. 'Mr and Mrs Ramsay? Would you bring Timothy this way, Dr Callaghan will see him now.'

Sara blushed in confusion, avoiding David's sardonic eyes, but Tim giggled in delight, and whispered loud enough that his uncle must have heard, 'I said I wanted you for a mother!'

In no time the doctor had removed the cast, talking such a stream of nonsense to the little boy that his nervousness was forgotten in laughter. Sara listened intently to Dr Callaghan's instructions, watching his blunt fingers rubbing and probing the wasted leg. He nodded his approval when she massaged the muscles, then showed Tim how to swing his knees alternatively from the edge of the high table, and how to flex his ankle and foot. 'That's fine, Sara. Very little weight on it for a day or two; get him standing between two chairs at first. Follow up with leg exercises to loosen up those stiff joints.' He grinned at Tim. 'You'll be playing football in ten days. If any problems come up, let me know. . .and if you ever want a job, Sara, let me know that too.'

'I'll be looking for one in September,' she admitted.

The doctor's tired face brightened. 'Will you, indeed? The hospital has the funds to pay a physiotherapist, but you just can't get girls to settle down here—not enough excitement, too far from the city, I've heard all the excuses. But I have a feeling you're different, Sara. Come along some time and we can discuss it further.'

'Thank you, Dr Callaghan,' she smiled. 'I'll certainly keep it in mind. Well, Tim, let's go home and get started, shall we?'

She was very conscientious about Tim's exercises the next two or three days, and had the gratification of seeing a steady improvement in him. This satisfaction balanced her unhappy conviction that David was avoiding her; when she did see him, his manner was distantly friendly, but more than once he took pains to steer clear of her altogether. Was she flattering herself to wonder if he was afraid of becoming too involved with her? She was sure he enjoyed her company, enjoyed it, moreover, on a deeper level than that of a casual social contact. But if so, why should he be evading her? Perhaps she was completely mistaken; perhaps those kisses had simply been a passing fancy, and he was still in love with the mysteriously departed Linda. After all, she knew very little of his earlier disastrous love affair. Painfully she recalled his contempt towards her that day at the falls— did he still think she was chasing him, wanting to add him to that imaginary collection of men? With a spurt of indignation that successfully covered the underlying hurt, she vowed to be as cool and detached as he. She would show him she didn't need his friendship!

On Sunday afternoon, he came to the Rutherfords' to

pick up Tim, and his granite features softened as with great concentration Tim walked unaided from the veranda to the car. He knelt to hug the boy, and unwillingly Sara was moved by the sight of the two tousled heads so close together. She would like to make the third of the little group, she confessed to herself, with a sharp sigh of annoyance at her own weakness.

Marilyn called from the doorway, 'Come in for a drink, David. You don't have to rush off, do you?'

To Sara's surprise, he accepted, and it was while they were sitting on the front lawn in the sun that they heard a car come down the driveway, signalling a loud tattoo with its horn. Harold jumped to his feet, pulling his wife up with him. 'Come on, darling, that's probably Charles.' A few moments later the three of them returned, laughing and talking at once in excitement.

Charles was taller and slimmer than his elder brother, his black hair immaculately groomed, his tanned face conventionally handsome. Marilyn introduced Sara to him, and his smile widened in spontaneous pleasure as he shook hands with her. 'Well, Harold, you didn't tell me I'd find anyone as exquisite as Sara in your rural retreat.'

His vitality and charm were so infectious, she couldn't help laughing. She dropped a mock curtsy and answered, 'Thank you, kind sir.' Beside her, David let out his breath in an audible hiss, but his voice was perfectly under control when he exchanged polite words of greeting with Charles. Shortly afterwards he excused himself, so Sara tactfully took Stephen and Patricia for a quick swim, leaving the Rutherfords alone to talk.

After dinner, when the children were in bed, they sat on the veranda in the evening cool, and Sara realised how much she was enjoying Charles's company—his open admiration and easy manner soothed her spirits, wounded by David's unpredictable behaviour. No hidden depths to Charles! He was as easy to read as a book, happy-go-lucky and fun-loving. She lightly parried his flirtatious remarks and contrived to forget David's absence, going to bed happier than she'd been since the night David had last kissed her.

On Monday, Marilyn and Harold took Charles golfing, from which he returned groaning theatrically, and complaining he hadn't walked so far in years. His body was lithe and athletic; as a result, Sara granted him little sympathy, even when he lamented, 'They dragged me over eighteen holes, up hill and down dale, over bridges, through forests and into sand traps, and all you can do is laugh.' Still grinning, he added, 'Would you come for a drive with me after dinner, Sara? I thought I'd go up the coast, Harold says the scenery is worth seeing.'

'I'd love to, provided Marilyn doesn't need me for the children. I'll go and check.'

Marilyn readily agreed. 'You've been busy lately, with Tim's therapy as well as our two on your hands. Have a good time.'

Charles opened the door of his shiny sedan for her, and Sara relaxed against the comfortable leather upholstery. Soft music came from the radio; the engine purred smoothly. Charles was a fast but very competent driver, handling the curves on the road with assurance. She found him a pleasant companion, with a fund of anecdotes about his European experiences.

At the age of ten, she had been to France and Holland with her father; since then, she'd always had a secret longing to return, particularly to the Netherlands. Charles had spent nearly a year based in Amsterdam. He rambled on about flower markets and museums, dykes and windmills, until she almost felt she was there again. She stirred in her seat, and Charles broke off. 'Am I boring you? Sorry, I loved the place, and do tend to flow on a bit when I get such a good audience.'

She smiled. 'No, I was far from bored. I must have been more tired than I realised—I haven't felt so peaceful and lazy for a long time. Please go on.'

He gave her an hilarious description of his first attempts at Alpine skiing, then suddenly pulled the car on to a grass verge, turning off the motor. They overlooked a rocky cove; the sun was setting on the horizon, colouring the clouds and the sea in a shimmer of pink and orange. A late gull swooped gracefully over the water. The only sound was the quiet splash of the tide.

Sara's throat tightened, for she was overwhelmed by a wave of longing to have David beside her to share this beauty. She was horrified by the intensity of this desire—what was wrong with her? How could she have let him gain such a hold over her?

She shivered a little, and Charles said solicitously, 'Cold? Here, throw my sweater around you.' He was sensitive enough to discern that something had upset her, so he turned the car around, and set himself to divert her. His gaiety was catching and Sara soon threw off her depression. She was chuckling at one of his witticisms as they walked to the house, his heavy sweater still about her shoulders. The laughter died on her lips when she saw David's rugged figure coming towards them; for the first time, she noticed his dark blue car parked by the side of the garage. He greeted them curtly, and even in the semi-darkness Sara could see that his eyes were brooding and bitter as they rested on her.

Her pleasure in the evening with Charles evaporated, and she excused herself as soon as she could. In the privacy of her room, she was dismayed to find tears running down her cheeks. She brushed them away with impatient fingers and, picking up a book, read until she was tired enough to sleep.

Tim's first swim of the summer took place the next day, carefully supervised by Sara. His excitement warmed her heart, for the bond between them was growing stronger every day, and it was an effort to ignore the niggling voice in the back of her mind that warned: don't get too fond of him—at the end of the summer you'll go your separate ways, and you might never see him again.

Oh, stop it, Sara, she told herself firmly. I don't know what's the matter with you, you're acting like a lovesick sixteen-year-old.

Determined to banish her confusing thoughts, she threw herself wholeheartedly into the children's games, and regained her usual serenity. At lunchtime, when Charles suggested a late dinner date at the resort hotel across the bay, she had no need to feign her pleasure. She experimented with a new hair-style, and dressed in her slim silk skirt, together with a halter top that bared her tanned arms and back.

The lights of the hotel glimmered gold in the dusk, while the scent of early roses hung on the air. 'We have time for a cocktail first,' Charles offered.

'Love one,' she agreed, again struck by his courtesy and thoughtfulness. He led her into the luxuriously appointed bar, where she sipped a Martini appreciatively, rather amused by the background of well-bred chatter from the elegant crowd of summer visitors. They made their way to the dining-room, and Sara studied the menu with frank enjoyment. 'I subsisted—that's the only word for it—on hospital food for two years in Montreal,' she explained to her escort. 'I never take food for granted now!' She finally decided on chilled Vichyssoise, poached salmon steak, and Viennese pastries; the meal was beautifully prepared, the waiter unobtrusive and highly efficient. Interested to know more about Charles,

Sara asked him about his work.

'I'm a public relations man for an insurance firm with branches across Europe—hence my six years over there. And I must admit I thoroughly enjoyed them. But even after Paris, Amsterdam and Zürich, it's rather nice to be back in Canada again; I should be at the head office in Toronto for at least a year.' He paused enquiringly. 'Are there any openings for physiotherapists in Toronto?'

She shook her head. 'Not for me, Charles. Two years in Montreal is enough of city rush and noise to do me for a while. As a matter of fact, I was offered a job the other day, by the surgeon at the local county hospital here.'

'Oh, Sara, you'd be burying yourself if you stayed here.'

To pacify him, she replied, 'I haven't taken it yet. The trouble is, I don't know where I want to go. I only know where I don't want to go, and that's not much help!'

Her companion's eyes were thoughtful as they dwelt on her fragile beauty in the glow of the candlelight, and on her ringless fingers. There must be something wrong with the men in this country, he mused. But for my sake, I'm glad she's unattached.

When they stepped out into the darkness, he slipped her stole around her shoulders; they drove slowly along the shore road for a while, before Charles turned down a lane to the sea, pulling up by the deserted beach. His arm was across the back of the seat behind her, and before she realised his intention he leaned over and kissed her expertly. Her lack of response acted as a challenge to him. He drew her closer with the adroitness of experience, and his mouth again claimed hers.

She recoiled instinctively, her body tense. 'Please don't, Charles.'

'Why not? You're an exceptionally pretty girl, the moon is rising, there's romance in the air. . .' He dropped his teasing manner, and said seriously, 'What's wrong? Is there someone else?'

'I don't know,' she answered miserably. Charles's skilful embrace had left her completely unmoved—she remembered the breathless sweetness that melted her body when David had kissed her. 'I'm sorry, Charles. I like you tremendously and I enjoy your company, but. . .I guess the chemistry's just not there.'

'But you know what's missing,' he continued perceptively. 'You're not so innocent that you haven't felt it with someone else.'

She nodded in confusion. 'I don't know why there should be such a difference.'

'Well, if you don't know, far be it from me to tell you. I won't give up hope, and we can still be friends.' He shook hands with her to seal the pact, and an uncertain smile wavered on her lips.

'I'm very glad to have you for a friend, Charles.'

He grinned crookedly. 'A pleasure, my lady. Now shall we go home, or would you like to go dancing? There's a big motel five miles away that operates a discothèque in the summer months.'

She considered, head on one side. 'Let's dance. I need to work off that huge—and delicious—dinner!'

They drove to the discothèque, a dimly lit cavern in the ground floor of the main lodge. Charles was an expert dancer, having an inborn feeling for music, and Sara was soon breathless. With his easy gregariousness, he struck up a conversation with another young couple, tourists from Vermont, and the four of them danced and talked until well past midnight. When he said goodnight to her at the Rutherfords', contenting himself with a warm handclasp, Sara was able to thank him for a lovely evening with perfect sincerity.

As usual, the next morning she and Marilyn had their

toast and coffee together in the kitchen. 'Did you enjoy yourself last night?' Marilyn asked.

'Yes, I did, Charles is great fun. We found every bright light in the village!' And she described their dinner, and the couple they had met at the discothèque.

'Oh, David phoned you while you were gone,' Marilyn mentioned casually. 'He has to go to Saraguay first thing this morning, and wondered if you'd look after Tim for him. I said I was sure you wouldn't mind—was I right?'

Sara tried to sound cool and impersonal. 'Of course, I'm always glad to see Tim,' she replied, with only a slight emphasis on the last word. Inwardly she resolved to keep out of sight when David delivered his nephew. Because she had promised to take the children fishing in the brook, they trooped out to the garden to dig some worms. She sat on the grass, her back against the old stone wall, breathing in the scent of honeysuckle, while Stephen dropped the worms, one by one, into a tin beside her. She regarded the wriggling mass with distaste. 'I hope you realise, Stephen, that I refuse to have anything to do with putting those on a hook, or with taking a fish off. Many things I will do for you, but not that.'

Stephen looked disgusted at such female squeamishness. 'Do you hear what she said, Tim?' he spluttered.

Sara turned her head to see Tim and David coming towards them on the other side of the wall. She received an instant impression that the man had been angry with her, but that somehow her remarks had lightened his mood.

'If you want to wait until after supper, I'll take you all fishing then,' he said coolly. 'The evening's a better time anyway.'

The children squealed with enthusiasm. 'Let's, Sara. Do say we can!'

TO TRUST MY LOVE

Conscious of amusement lurking behind David's eyes, she accepted ungraciously. 'That's very kind of you.' This was the second time he'd put her on the spot!

'I'll fetch you about six o'clock, then. Keep the worms in the shade, Stephen.'

Sara watched him drive up the lane, wondering how one man could cause her such a turmoil of conflict emotion whenever she saw him. It simply wasn't fair. . .she wished she could believe he wanted her company this evening, but it was obviously meant as a treat for the children.

After a lazy day on the beach, they hurriedly ate their dinner, and dressed in trousers and long-sleeved shirts. Sara carefully rubbed insect repellant on the children's exposed skin, to ward off mosquitoes, then helped them gather their rods and paraphernalia. They were all waiting when David swung down the driveway in his battered jeep, a fibre-glass rowing boat strapped to the top. He was wearing fishing boots and old khaki trousers; her heart skipped a beat as she recognised the red-checked shirt as the one he had been wearing on their first meeting—the button was still missing from it.

They piled into the cramped seats of the jeep, Patricia on Sara's lap, and the two boys in the back on a pile of life-jackets. The latter's high spirits were contagious, and when David's eye caught Sara's they grinned at each other spontaneously. 'Are we all here?' he shouted above the racket. 'Away we go!'

Reaching for the gear-shift, his hand brushed Sara's leg, and she flushed, disturbed by the warmth of his body; their shoulders rubbed together as they lurched up the drive and on to the main road. He explained above the roar of the motor that the jeep was rather temperamental, and had to be treated with respect—certainly, it gave her the impression of being held together with string and hope. However, they reached the lake without mishap, and parked by the rocky shore. After David untied the boat, he and Sara righted it on the ground. The children were bundled into life-jackets, and they pushed off, David rowing, Sara facing him in the bow, the little girl beside her. Once they were away from the shore, David shipped the oars, in order to help Patricia with her tiny rod.

The lake was clear and still, bird song rang from the circle of surrounded hills, and the fishing lines splashed gently on the water. In a flurry of excitement, Stephen soon hauled in a small trout; Sara averted her eyes as David swiftly killed it. He glanced over at her. 'Sorry, Sara, but it's better to do it that way than to leave it gasping for air in the bottom of the boat.'

'Yes, I know, it's silly of me.'

Quiet descended again, and half an hour passed before Tim got a bite. He reeled the fish in, its body arching and fighting above the water, and was delighted to land a ten-inch speckled trout.

The sun was sinking behind the hills in a blaze of gold, so David rowed slowly back to the landing, where they packed the gear away, and lifted the dripping boat back on to the vehicle. The evening calm was suddenly broken by a series of faraway, bloodcurdling cries. Her eyes wide with alarm, Sara gasped, 'What's that, David?'

'Don't worry, no one's been murdered,' he reassured her, resting a casual hand on her sleeve. 'It's a loon. Have you never heard one before?' They listened intently while the weird sound echoed again, ending in a high-pitched tremolo. His words fell softly in the twilight air. 'We're lucky to hear them, they're becoming increasingly rare. The loon's a waterbird that needs peace and quiet, and won't nest near human habitation; motorboats are anathema to it. Its cry is one of the authentic thrills of the wilderness.' He looked down at his nephew. 'You'd better read about them in your bird book.'

He dropped Sara and her two charges off at the Rutherfords', but wouldn't stay. 'Bedtime for this fellow,' he explained, affectionately ruffling Tim's hair. 'I enjoyed it too,' was his reply, looking straight at Sara as he said it, a challenge in his direct gaze.

'Give me your shirt some time, and I'll sew the button on for you,' she offered, her grey eyes still soft with the peace of the lake and the wonder of the loon's cry. The memory of his parting smile kindled a hope in her breast that he would not again retreat from her friendship. Surely, in time, he would forget the girl in his past. . .

As it happened, she was shortly to learn more about Linda. Marilyn was full of energy at breakfast the next morning. 'Let's go picking wild strawberries, Sara. It's an ideal day, a breeze to keep the mosquitoes away and it's not too hot yet. One of the few domestic things I do every summer is make jam out of the berries. Harold swears he'd walk twenty miles for it, so I know it must be good! He'll keep an eye on the children, if you'd like to come.'

'Sounds lovely. Uncle Matthew and I always used to pick them at home; they taste so much better than the cultivated ones, don't they?'

Equipped with plastic containers and sunhats, they drove three or four miles to a deserted farm. The fields were edged with birch and maple, and generously sprinkled with daisies and sweet-smelling clover. Marilyn dropped to her knees. 'They're all through the grass here. Look, Sara, they're perfect.'

In a companionable silence, they began to pick, the small scarlet berries staining their fingers. 'We should have brought David,' Marilyn lamented. 'He's an avid berry picker, lots of patience. I can remember he took Linda once—but only once! Her manicure was ruined and the mosquitoes spoiled her complexion. Mind you, she was a real beauty, and still is, if I know Linda. She's one of the few people Harold and I have ever disagreed on. He thought she was marvellous, and just the wife for David, but I could never see it.'

She straightened her back, wrinkling her retroussé nose in thought. 'She was like a hothouse flower, flamboyant and exotic, but needing a very protected environment to survive. Wealth, good family, plenty of admirers, a small army of hairdressers, maids, dress-designers—she simply didn't fit David's lifestyle, but he was too much in love to realise that. I still think she'd have led him a merry dance if he'd married her.'

Her fingers busy among the delicate plants, Sara listened with mixed feelings. How could she, Sara, hope to replace the 'flamboyant and exotic' Linda? Yet it was her own natural looks and love of the outdoors that seemed to appeal to David. She gave up trying to solve the riddle, and moved to another patch of berries, noting with satisfaction how her bowl was slowly filling.

They picked for another hour before Marilyn got to her feet with a mock groan. 'My knees have had it, I must be getting old. Besides, it's too hot, and the flies are eating me alive. Let's call it a day. I can make the jam this evening, when it's cooler.'

When they got home, Harold, Charles and David were reclining lazily in lawn chairs, mugs of cold beer beside them, the three children busy with a game of croquet. Marilyn scowled darkly at her husband. 'I always said it was a man's world.'

'Whatever you say, darling. It's too hot to argue.' He patted the arm of his chair. 'Sit down and have a beer, instead.'

David stood up, laughing. 'I'll be more polite, and give you a seat, Sara. Hey, what gorgeous berries! There's a big patch behind my house. You'll have to come and help me pick them.'

Marilyn intervened. 'She's worse than you, David, I'm sure she'd have stayed there all day. But if you want to pick them, I'll make the jam for you.'

'We'll never get another offer like that,' David bantered. 'How about tomorrow morning? Is seven too early, Sara? We could be back by nine.'

'I'd love to.' She pushed a wisp of dark hair off her warm face. 'I hope it's not as hot as today, though.'

Standing very close to her, he tucked another stray strand behind her ear. She felt her skin tingle; her thick lashes fluttered down over her grey eyes, hiding their traitorous happiness from his penetrating blue ones. Harold loudly knocked over an ashtray behind them, they moved hastily apart, and the moment of intimacy passed. David offered her a beer, and the conversation became general.

In the fresh beauty of the early morning, serenaded by a chorus of birdsong, Sara threaded through the woods to David's. She emerged from the trees into a patch of sunlight, just as he came down the steps. 'Good morning,' he said quietly. 'Tim is still asleep, I told him last night where we'd be. Listen to the birds!'

'There's really no excuse for staying in bed late in the summer, is there?' she teased wickedly, remembering more than one morning when he'd been quite late delivering Tim to play with Stephen.

'Touché!' he laughed. 'Your turn will come.'

Side by side in the dew-spangled field, they gathered the ripe red fruit. The time passed all too quickly, and they were about to leave when Sara suddenly laid her hand on David's bare forearm. He glanced down at her, not attempting to hide his pleasure at this spontaneous gesture.

'Look,' she whispered, 'over there by the old orchard.' Her fingers unconsciously dug into his flesh in excitement, as a doe and her white-spotted fawn moved slowly across the meadow, cropping the lush grass, their tails swishing at the flies.

'The fawn's only about three months old,' David murmured into her ear. 'They're such delicate-looking creatures, aren't they, but they're tough enough to live through the long winter of ice and snow.'

The doe raised her head, ears pricked, then gave a snort of alarm as a wayward breeze carried their scent to her. With a flick of her white tail, the two deer disappeared into the undergrowth.

Sara released her pent-up breath in a long sigh of pure enchantment. 'To see a wild creature free in its own surroundings never fails to fascinate me,' she said. 'I hate zoos and loathe seeing animals in cages, don't you?'

He nodded in agreement, his eyes tender and amused when, realising her hand was still clasping his arm, she jerked it away in confusion. 'I'd better make sure Tim's all right, then I'll drive you home,' he said. In perfect harmony with each other, they made their way to the house, his arm draped casually across her shoulders.

As he went in the back door, she wished with a mingled rush of longing and disappointment that he had kissed her. She had a feeling he was waiting for something, biding his time. . .and yet she was sure he liked her, was perhaps even on the brink of loving her.

And what of herself? With a wonder as fresh as the dawn, she knew she loved this man, and had loved him from the beginning. Momentarily she was shocked by this revelation—she'd been too innocent to realise the depth of her commitment to him. Oh, David, David. . .

TO TRUST MY LOVE

Was he totally unmoved by her presence? Could it be only her heartbeat that quickened at their closeness?

She ruefully recalled some of her friend Joan's advice from their Montreal days; Joan's sophisticated savoir-faire would soon find a way to cajole a kiss. Yet deep within her, she was convinced that her tenuous relationship with David could be ruined by feminine wiles and manipulation. He put a high value on honesty. She would simply have to be herself and be patient. . .

CHAPTER SIX

IT WAS three days later, and Sara woke feeling uncharacteristically sorry for herself. Today was her birthday—she was twenty-four years old. Both her father and Uncle Matthew had been firm believers in celebrating birthdays, managing to make each one memorable in some special way. Dear Uncle Matthew. . . Yesterday she had received cards from Miss Rutherford, and from Joan and Simon, Joan's containing an impatiently awaited letter which had been very encouraging as far as Simon's progress was concerned. And that was all she could expect. No one here knew it was her birthday, so it would be a day like any other.

Her drooping spirits revived when she pulled back the curtains; the sky was a cloudless, eggshell blue, promising heat to come. After all, she could have been back in her cramped room in the hospital, in the humidity and noise of a Montreal July. Dressing in brief green shorts and a striped top, she wondered if the children were up—they were very quiet. She made her way to the kitchen, where she halted in amazement as Stephen and Patricia cried, 'Happy birthday, Sara,' and Marilyn warmly repeated the sentiment.

'But. . .but how did you know?' she stammered. 'I didn't tell anyone.'

Stephen grinned triumphantly. 'Remember the day you dropped your wallet, and all your cards fell out? I was the one who picked up your driver's licence and I saw your birthday on it; I wrote it down so we wouldn't forget it.'

He looked so pleased with himself that Sara dropped a quick kiss on his red hair, admitting, 'I was feeling rather sorry for myself because nobody would know today was my birthday.'

Marilyn smiled. 'We have it all planned. David and Tim are coming over after lunch, and we'll all have a swim. Then there is to be a dinner party at the Rutherford residence in your honour at seven o'clock!'

'That sounds lovely,' Sara assured her, touched by her friend's kindness.

That afternoon, though she would have vehemently denied it, it was because David was outside that she decided against wearing her usual rather faded one-piece swimsuit. She had made herself a bikini out of a brightly coloured floral print, which she had not yet had the courage to wear. It was her first attempt at a bathing suit, and although it fitted her slim body to perfection, it revealed considerably more of Sara than she had intended. She had sewn a matching beach coat, so she pulled this on over the bikini and gathered her hair back with a ribbon.

When she joined the others on the beach, she felt suddenly shy as she slipped off her jacket, and blushed as Charles gave a long, appreciative wolf whistle. But it was David's gaze she sought, and again they experienced one of those fleeting moments of intimacy that set her pulses racing, for his blue eyes had a spark of flame in their depths. He jumped to his feet, and grabbed her by the hand. 'Come on, time for a swim!'

Hand in hand, they ran down the sand, splashing waist-deep into the sea, then letting the waves buffet their bodies. For all that it was July, there was an invigorating chill to the water that made movement imperative. Sara plunged through a foam-crested wave; with a smooth overarm crawl, she swam away from the shore, David in close pursuit.

Once he was out of his depth, he dived to the sandy bottom, finally surfacing with a tiny white pebble in his hand. Treading water, laughter lines creasing around his eyes, he offered it to Sara. 'Accept this gift of a pearl beyond price, o, beautiful lady!'

'David, you are a fool,' she giggled, trying not to swallow the water slapping at her chin. Surely he had never looked so handsome—his wheat-gold hair in soaked curls, his white teeth gleaming, droplets of water on his tanned shoulders, his eyes the colour of the restless sea. To relieve her feelings, she splashed him vigorously. Twisting away from his vengeful lunge, she took a deep breath and dived beneath the surface. She opened her eyes to find herself in another world, a world of waving seaweed and dim green light, in which David's body was swimming towards her, his muscles rippling under his skin. Mischievously, she waited until he almost reached her before she eluded him, her limbs weightless and graceful, her hair floating in a dark cloud about her head. Then, her lungs aching for air, she propelled herself to the surface.

A strong arm encircled her. His face alight with laughter, David panted, 'Why, whenever I want to kiss you, are you soaking wet?'

His cold lips found hers; they floated to the crest of the swell, and Charles's voice shouted, 'None of that, you two! Come and help me control these three little ruffians.'

A wet game of catch ensued, Tim able to jump and swim with the rest of them. Sara was breathless as she rejoined the Rutherfords, picked up her towel, and wiped the salt drops from her face. 'Aren't you going in, Marilyn? After the initial shock, it's gorgeous!'

'No, it has to be much warmer for Harold and me,' she

replied, with a grimace at her recumbent husband.

Chuckling, Sara spread her towel on the warm sand, and fell silent while she watched the antics of the others in the sea, her eyes lingering on David's tall figure. She was bound to this man, bound by ties stronger than steel. It wasn't only his physical attractiveness, his rugged masculinity that set her pulses racing; she was also deeply aware of his basic goodness and strength, convinced that the woman he loved would find security and an abiding happiness with him. Somehow his emotions had become padlocked behind a wall of reserve, but surely the gate could be opened—if only it could be she who did this. . . The heat of the sun soaked into her skin, and she lay back with a sigh of contentment.

A body thudded into the sand beside her; she hid her disappointment when she saw it was Charles. 'Having a nice day?' he asked, continuing without waiting for an answer, 'Why do David's hackles rise every time I come near you?'

With an effort, Sara managed to say calmly, 'Do they? I hadn't noticed,' hoping she would be forgiven the untruth.

'You mean you didn't see the murderous look he gave me, when I whistled at your very charming swimsuit? If looks could kill, I wouldn't be here now.'

'Don't be silly, Charles, you're exaggerating,' she scolded, and turned over on her stomach with her face buried in her towel. Charles saw altogether too much, she thought, and she didn't trust him an inch.

She sang softly to herself while she showered and dressed for dinner, choosing a plain white sundress, her tanned arms and legs bare, her wrist encircled with a heavy silver bracelet that had been her mother's. They were all gathered in the dining-room waiting for her, and the pile of gaily wrapped parcels by her seat brought a lump to her throat. The children hovered around her, obviously anxious for her to open them. 'Start with mine,' said Patricia, handing her an untidy package held together with liberal quantities of tape and ribbon.

The little girl had made her an ornament of shells and starfish glued to a piece of driftwood; Stephen had bought chocolates, and Tim had sketched and painted a pair of warblers on a spruce bough. She thanked each of them, impressed by their thoughtfulness, then pulled at the paper on Charles's tiny gift: a flaçon of extremely expensive French perfume. She sprayed it on her wrist and inhaled with delight. 'Mmm, that's heavenly, Charles, thank you. I've coveted that brand of perfume for years.'

There was a large, beautifully wrapped box from Marilyn and Harold; with a flutter of anticipation, she lifted the lid, then stammered incoherently, 'Oh, Marilyn, you shouldn't have, it's too much. But it's absolutely gorgeous.' It was a dark green suede jacket, the skin soft and supple, a matching Liberty scarf tucked in the neckline. She tried it on, and paraded around the room, mocking the stage walk of a model, a glow of excitement on her cheeks. Impulsively she dropped a kiss on Marilyn's cheek. 'Thank you both so much, you're far too good to me.'

'Not a bit of it,' disclaimed Harold. 'You're one of the family now.'

Sara had left David's present until the last. She picked it up experimentally, but apart from being flat and rather heavy, it gave no clue as to the contents. Her fingers slightly unsteady, she opened the card, which was inscribed simply, 'To Sara, with gratitude and love, David and Timothy.' Inside the box was a painting, a painting with the same vigorous masculinity of the one on her wall. It depicted the Point in a storm, grey seas dashing against the cliffs, spruce trees bent in the gale, a cloudy and windswept sky. Sara was quite unable to say a word, and could only gaze at David, her heart in her eyes, finally whispering huskily, 'Thank you, David. You couldn't have given me anything I would have liked better.'

Harold cleared his throat, lessening the emotional tension in the room, while the children all started to talk at once, giving the girl a chance to regain her composure. Marilyn had planned a dinner of Sara's favourites: lobster fresh from the ocean, crisp salads and homemade rolls. Harold ceremoniously brought in the birthday cake, the candles flickering in the dusk, and as they all sang 'Happy birthday', Sara felt as though she did indeed belong in this family.

After the children were in bed, Tim sleeping on the extra bunk in Stephen's room, the five adults sat lazily in the living-room, replete with sunshine and Mrs Donnelly's excellent cooking. Marilyn at last said, sleepily repressing a yawn, 'Oh, goodness, I'm a terrible hostess, Sara! The golf tournament opens at nine o'clock tomorrow morning, so Harold and I will have to be up early. Will you excuse us, please?'

'Of course, and thank you both again. It was a wonderful day from beginning to end.'

Charles also got up, and stretched with a slightly exaggerated yawn. 'I'm expected to be there bright and early tomorrow to cheer Harold on, so perhaps I'd better hit the sack, as well. Goodnight, David, Sara.' Impishly, he winked at the girl as he lightly kissed her forehead. 'Many more happy birthdays, honey.'

She grimaced at him, and replied with dignity, 'Thank you, Charles. Goodnight.' Wretched man—he knew David was quizzically watching the pair of them. She turned to find David standing behind her.

'Perhaps I'd better go too. I have a deadline to meet on an article I haven't even started yet. I'll have to get on with it tomorrow, or I'll have the editor breathing down my neck. However, I have a plan for Saturday. I've been feeling a bit guilty that Tim's taken up so much of your spare time, so Marilyn and I got our heads together—she'll be happy to look after all three children, and you and I could spend the day somewhere. I wondered if you'd like to go into the interior, the scenery's fascinating, very different from the coast. Although the road's not the best, I'm sure the jeep could manage it. Would you like to do that, or would you prefer a day shopping in Saraguay?'

'Oh, no. I'd much rather a day in the outdoors.'

'Wonderful! Wear trousers and comfortable walking shoes, I'll look after everything else.' His voice deepened. 'And now I really must go. If I stay here with you beside me, and the moonlight coming in the window, heaven knows what will happen. If I may be guilty of quoting a romantic poet, Sara, you too walk in beauty like the night.'

She blushed as he took her hands in his firm clasp, gently playing with her fingers. 'David, the painting is beautiful, I'll always treasure it.'

'And you are the nicest gift the summer could have brought me. You're so dependable and trustworthy. I suppose that doesn't sound very romantic, does it? But you can't imagine how wonderful it is to find I can trust a woman again. You're healing something that's been broken for three years.'

Profoundly stirred, she said, 'I'm so glad, David.'

His mouth curved in a smile as he bent his head to kiss her. Her heart thudded painfully in her breast; his arms came around her and their lips met, her hands shyly stealing up behind his neck. Slowly he released her, a pulse beating hard in his throat. 'Goodnight, my beautiful Sara,' he whispered. For a moment, he laid his face against the shining fragrance of her hair, then he was gone.

In a daze of happiness, Sara watched his car lights disappear up the driveway. She wandered dreamily to the window, gazing out at the stars. To think she had dreaded this birthday, and longed for it to be over. Instead, it had reinforced her love for David, reinforced her conviction that he was falling in love with her. Not even the episode of Linda's photograph seemed so threatening now; with new-found confidence, Sara was sure she could make him forget Linda.

She picked up the painting from the table, her fingers caressing the frame, and carried it to her room. Tomorrow, she'd get a picture hook from Harold, and hang it above the bookshelves. She breathed a silent prayer of thanksgiving that she'd been fortunate enough to find these warm-heared people—they had certainly given her a birthday to remember.

She awoke early on the Saturday morning, and lay there for a while, filled with the joy of her secret love. Humming quietly, she pulled on blue jeans and a cotton shirt. A whole day alone with David. . .she couldn't believe he was asking her merely to make amends for the time she had spent with Tim.

The two of them drove off in the jeep, David explaining the route as he went. 'We go almost to the falls, then turn inland; we can drive about eight miles before the road gets too rough even for this old crate.'

When she saw the turn-off, she decided his words were an understatement. It was a dirt track wide enough for only one vehicle, overhung by tree limbs and in places eroded by rain to the bare rock. David drove at what seemed to her a reckless pace, and she grabbed her seat for support as they rocketed up a slope, loose stones spinning under the tyres. He laughed, and rested a casual hand on her knee. 'Don't worry, I could drive this road with my eyes shut.'

She firmly replaced his hand on the wheel. 'Please don't. And I'm sure you need both hands to steer.' She shuddered as they rounded a turn, and he slammed on the brakes.

'I'm glad I didn't hit them—look!'

She opened her eyes, which widened with delight; a mother partridge was sedately chivvying her brood of fluffy chicks over the bank, into the concealing undergrowth. David drove more slowly after that, pointing out how they were leaving the trees behind. 'There's so little soil over the bedrock that only low-growing shrubs and mosses can survive. It's a bleak place in winter, no shelter from the wind at all. My brother and I snowshoed up here one January, it was like another world.'

Curious about his family, she asked, 'Are your parents living, David?'

'My father's been dead for several years. He was a most astute businessman, and left James and me very well off. I think he was a bit disappointed neither of us followed his footsteps—James was an engineer. My mother lives in Rochford; she values her independence and is determined to leave me mine. She's chairman of so many committees, I don't know how she keeps them all straight. Mind you, they're all worth-while, she'd be sure of that.' He broke off. 'I think we've gone about as far as we can. Do you feel like walking? There's a lake on the other side of that hill, we might be lucky enough to catch ourselves a late lunch.'

She nodded eagerly, and they set off. David led the way, occasionally reaching back to help her over a rough spot. That enchanted day was always to remain in Sara's memory. As her vision swept over the lonely rock-strewn hills that sprawled to the horizon, she knew she would be frightened to be here alone, but it was obvious David was very much at home in these desolate surroundings, and she felt perfectly safe with him. His intimate knowledge of the plant and animal life that flourished in this harsh environment impressed her, as did the easy skill with which he landed four gleaming speckled trout.

He built a small fire on the shore, his face peaceful and relaxed as he fed dry wood to the greedy flames; Sara didn't think she had ever tasted anything so delicious as those delicate pink fillets, crisp and hot from the pan. She leaned back with a sigh of repletion, and David smiled at her, an uncomplicated smile of pleasure at sharing his beloved outdoors with one who appreciated it. Feeling a betraying blush flood her cheeks, she busied herself ladling sugar and powdered milk into the coffee mugs, and they drank in a contented silence, the ripple of the lake water and the distant peeping of a sandpiper the only sounds to be heard.

Afterwards, David lay back on the ground, his jacket rolled up as a pillow under his head. 'Wake me in half an hour,' he requested drowsily. His eyelids closed, and almost at once his breathing became deep and regular. For a while, Sara sat quietly beside him, thinking that he had been working too hard lately, and could well do with a day of rest, away from the self-imposed pressures of his writing. She studied his sleeping face with secret delight—they could be alone in the world in this primitive and beautiful place.

She stretched lazily, then rolled her jeans above her knees and paddled into the lake to scour out the dishes with sand. After setting them to dry on a rock, she splashed her way along the shore, unsuccessfully trying to catch the slippery tadpoles in her fingers, and admiring the waxy cream and pink waterlilies that bobbed on the surface.

Cautiously rounding a promontory, she froze into stillness. A loon, its chick nestled on its back, was slowly gliding across the cove. Even as she watched, its mate reappeared above the surface, then smoothly dived again in its search for food. Utterly fascinated, and quite oblivious of the passage of time, she observed them, admiring their sleek, black and white plumage and graceful movements.

'Sara! Where are you?'

David's anxious shout roused her from her absorption. She was unwilling to disturb the shy birds, so she ducked behind a rock and, doubled over, crossed to the next little inlet, before straightening and calling, 'I'm over here!'

He loped along the water's edge to meet her. 'You had me worried, I couldn't see you anywhere. Do you know you let me sleep for over two hours?'

'Oh, David, you're joking,' she said in blank amazement. 'I was watching a pair of loons with their chick, and I guess I lost track of the time completely.'

'They nested here? That's great. There's only one pair to a lake, they're very territory-conscious.' He stopped his scientific explanations, and grinned at her carefully picking her way over the rocks towards him in bare feet. 'You look about sixteen in that rig.'

Somehow his arms came around her. Her heart began to pound as he said softly, 'Beautiful Sara.' His first kiss was gentle, but her shy response unleashed his dammed-up passion. Crushed by his strength as his ardent lips met hers, she was pervaded by an answering fire that threatened to consume her, an ecstasy of longing that left her weak. Her slight body was trembling when his grip finally loosened; her eyes were dark with the sensuous wonder of that awakening, for she had been swept by sensations she had never felt before.

He smoothed back her hair with a hand that shook slightly. 'We'd better go back,' he said huskily. 'I won't be accountable for what happens if I kiss you again. You're so sweet and innocent, Sara, I'd given up hope of ever finding anyone like you.' He buried his face in her neck, the skin warm and delicately scented; he could feel a pulse racing in her throat. With an inarticulate groan, he swung her into his arms, and carried her back along the shore to the dead embers of the camp fire, where he released her with deliberate restraint. 'Put your shoes on, sweetheart, they're by my jacket. I'll throw a bit of water on the ashes, just to make sure they're out.' They wandered along the trail to the jeep, hand in hand; evening was falling and the air was still, bathed in a golden light.

It was dusk when they reached home. After he had gone, Sara excused herself. She ran a steaming hot bath, letting her mind dwell on each moment of that perfect day. And yet had it been quite perfect? For the first time, she openly admitted to herself the tiny doubt that was nibbling at her peace of mind—David had never mentioned the word 'love', never uttered those magic words. 'I love you.' Why should he hold back? Unless she was completely mistaken in her reading of his character, he must surely love her to kiss her as he had. Did he not realise from her response that she was in love with him? He couldn't believe their mutual desire was based only on a physical attraction! She had longed to tell him that she had never experienced a kiss like that before, that she had been unaware of the fires slumbering in her body. But how could she, when she wasn't sure of his feelings towards her?

Stop it, Sara, she mentally reprimanded herself. Trust

him, that's all you can do. Pushing her uncertainty to the back of her mind, she fell into bed, and, with the memory of David's arms around her, drifted to sleep.

FREE BOOKS!

FREE GIFTS!

PLAY THE "LUCKY 7" SLOT MACHINE GAME!

AND YOU COULD GET FREE BOOKS, A FREE CUDDLY TEDDY AND A SURPRISE GIFT!

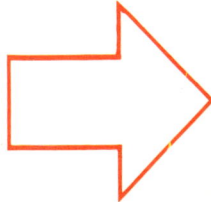

NO COST! NO OBLIGATION TO BUY! NO PURCHASE NECESSARY!

PLAY "LUCKY 7" AND GET AS MANY AS SIX FREE GIFTS...

HOW TO PLAY:

1. With a coin, carefully scratch off the silver box opposite. You will now be eligible to receive one or more free books, and possibly other gifts, depending on what is revealed beneath the scratch off area.

2. When you return this card, you'll receive specially selected Mills & Boon Romances. We'll send you the books and gifts you qualify for **absolutely free**, and at the same time we'll reserve you a subscription to our Reader Service.

3. If we don't hear from you, we'll then send you six brand new Romances to read and enjoy every month for just £1.60 each, the same price as the books in the shops.
There is no extra charge for postage and handling.
There are no hidden extras.

4. When you join the Mills & Boon Reader Service, you'll also get our free monthly Newsletter; featuring author news, horoscopes, penfriends and competitions.

5. You are under no obligation, and may cancel or suspend your subscription at any time simply by writing to us.

You'll love your cuddly teddy. His brown eyes and cute face are sure to make you smile.

PLAY "LUCKY 7"

Just scratch off the silver box with a coin.
Then check below to see which gifts you get.

YES! I have scratched off the silver box. Please send me all the gifts for which I qualify. I understand I am under no obligation to purchase any books, as explained on the opposite page. I am over 18 years of age.

MS/MRS/MISS/MR   2A2R

ADDRESS

POSTCODE   SIGNATURE

7 7 7	WORTH FOUR FREE BOOKS, FREE TEDDY BEAR AND MYSTERY GIFT
🍒 🍒 🍒	WORTH FOUR FREE BOOKS AND MYSTERY GIFT
🌰 🌰 🌰	WORTH FOUR FREE BOOKS
🔔 🔔 🍒	WORTH TWO FREE BOOKS

Offer expires 31st May 1992. The right is reserved to change the terms of this offer or refuse an application. Readers overseas and in Eire please send for details. Southern Africa write to Book Services International Ltd., P.O. Box 41654, Craighall, Transvaal 2024. You may be mailed with offers from other reputable companies as a result of this application. If you would prefer not to share in this opportunity please tick box. ☐

MILLS & BOON "NO RISK" GUARANTEE
- You're not required to buy a single book—ever!
- You must be completely satisfied or you may cancel at any time simply by writing to us. You will receive no more books; you'll have no further obligation.
- The free books and gifts you receive from this "Lucky 7" offer remain yours to keep no matter what you decide.

If offer card is missing, write to:
Mills & Boon Reader Service, Freepost, P.O. Box 236, Croydon, Surrey CR9 9EL

Mills & Boon Reader Service
Freepost
P.O. Box 236
Croydon
Surrey
CR9 9EL

No Stamp Needed

CHAPTER SEVEN

MATCHING the contentment of Sara's mood, the slow July days idled by, hot and sunny. Marilyn and Harold were busily involved with the golf tournament, and Charles was gone with them most of the time. She and the children swam and played on the beach; even Tim's increasing dependence on her didn't disturb her serenity—perhaps it would turn out for the best.

Because David was working hard on his magazine article, she saw little of him. It was several days after her party, at one of their brief meetings, that he admitted to her ruefully, 'It's not going nearly as well as I thought it would.' Exasperated, he ran his fingers through his already untidy hair. 'It's a damn nuisance, but I'll have to spend tomorrow in the Saraguay library. I can't think of anything worse in this heat. I'm really neglecting Tim, but he's obviously very happy in your company. I'm getting jealous, you know,' he teased, his smile smoothing away the tired lines on his face.

He rested his hands on her bare shoulders, warm from the sun, and at his touch, a delicious weakness invaded her limbs. 'I haven't seen much of you lately,' he apologised. 'I shouldn't let myself get so bogged down in these wretched articles, the summer's too short. Especially this summer. . .' On the brink of saying something further, he hesitated, and the moment was lost. The tiny flicker of hope in Sara's breast died away. 'I probably won't be home tomorrow until nine or ten in the evening; maybe we could go for a walk then, hmm?'

'I'd love that,' she promised, her clear grey eyes

shining up at him. 'I'll wait for you here.'

The next day was scorchingly hot, Sara and the children were all sitting in the shade of the house sipping ice-cold lemonade, when Harold's car rolled down the drive and a very wilted trio emerged. 'You've got the right idea, Sara,' Marilyn panted. 'Phew, it was hot on the greens, not a breath of wind. I love golf, but I'm not sorry to see the end of that tournament.'

Charles flopped on the lawn beside them. 'I'm surfeited with the cursed game, it's coming out of my ears. I never want to see a five-iron again.' He lay back on the grass, immaculately groomed as always, his black hair sleek, and Sara smiled down at him. He was a nice person, she thought, not as mature and steady as Harold, but then he was a lot younger. He winked at her. 'What are you thinking behind that enigmatic smile? I'll tell you what I'm thinking. Let's take a picnic, drive somewhere up the shore, and eat by the sea. There'll be a breeze coming up soon, and I could sure do with one—it's been a stifling day. Will you come? You're more or less off duty at five, aren't you?'

'Oh, I don't know, Charles.' Sara sounded uncertain, as she rapidly hunted for an excuse. 'Marilyn probably wants to rest, and I could take the children off her hands for a while longer.'

'You're far too conscientious,' Charles argued. 'I'll speak to Marilyn, she won't mind. Or don't you want to go?'

She hesitated momentarily, then decided honesty was the best policy. 'A bit of peace and quiet sounds terrific, it's been a long, hot day. But you see, I promised David I'd be here when he gets back from Saraguay and I wouldn't want to disappoint him.'

She blushed at Charles's sardonic look and derisive comment. 'So that's the way the wind's blowing, is it?

Far be it for me to impede the progress of romance. I guarantee I'll have you home by eight, how would that be?'

She surrendered, laughing. 'You've very persuasive. If it's all right with Marilyn, I'd love to go.'

They went into the kitchen, where Mrs Donnelly and Marilyn had just poured themselves iced tea. 'Help yourselves,' Marilyn invited. 'Sara dear, why don't you take the car and disappear for a while? You've been a real saint these last few days.'

Charles chuckled, congratulating his sister-in-law, 'Hey, you and I are on the same wavelength. I've just been trying to persuade her we should take a picnic and find somewhere cool to eat, and she's been telling me she can't leave her job.'

Mrs Donnelly spoke up. 'I have cold chicken and lettuce I can wrap up for you, with fresh rolls, fruit and cake. How would that be?'

'Wonderful! Bless you, Mrs D. I'll be ready in a minute, Charles.' Sara went to get her swimsuit, thinking she would be glad of an hour or so away; the children had been listless and hard to please in the heat, and, too, it wouldn't seem so long to wait until she saw David again. She wondered if she should leave him a note, then decided against it; Charles had promised she'd be home by eight.

The car picked up speed on the highway, the wind whipping her hair about her ears, and she gratefully acknowledged, 'This was a good idea of yours, Charles. Where are we going?'

'You'll see,' he replied. 'I've just had a brainwave.'

She reclined against the smooth leather of the seat and let her thoughts drift. It must have been a hot day for David in the city; she hoped he wouldn't be too tired. It was surely a good sign that he wanted her to be waiting for him on his return. . .she emerged from her daydreams to find the car jolting down a dirt track to an old wharf. 'Where on earth are we?'

Her companion grinned at her, his teeth white in his tanned, conventionally handsome face. 'Johnson's wharf. I was talking to one of the fishermen the other day, and he told me I could have his boat any evening this week. We'll go out to Bear Island, it's only a mile or so away.' And he indicated the tree-clad island off-shore, fringed with white sand and rippling surf. 'That's his boat, moored by the ladder. Better throw your sweater in, it can turn cold quickly on the sea.'

He climbed down the ladder, took the picnic basket from Sara, and helped her into the boat. 'It's not the most modern vessel in the world, is it? But it's difficult to get one at all in lobster season. I hope I can figure out this engine, it's a bit of a museum piece, to say the least.'

To Sara, it looked totally inoperable, but in less than five minutes it was vibrating with a steady hum and they pulled away from the wharf, wending their way carefully through the jagged rocks. The sea sparkled in the sun; a pair of terns swooped gracefully overhead as they approached the island. Charles cut the engine, and the little boat drifted into shore, waves slapping sharply against the prow. For Sara, the untouched beauty of the deserted beach needed only David's presence to make it perfect.

After they had swum in the crystal clear water, they attacked Mrs Donnelly's food with sharpened appetites. 'I'm so glad I came, Charles,' Sara confessed. 'I guess I was feeling a bit housebound, without really realising it. This is a gorgeous place.'

He looked at her shrewdly, a shadow of regret in his expression. 'You'll have to come back here with David.'

She jumped to her feet, pulling a rude face at him. 'That's the second time I've decided you see altogether too much, Charles Rutherford. I'm going to get dressed, it's cooling off. Should we be leaving soon?'

'Lord, yes, it's nearly eight. It'll be dark before we know it. Oh, well, it won't take us long to get home.'

Clad in jeans and sweater, Sara left the shelter of the thick trees, and gathered up the picnic things, wondering uneasily why the engine was emitting those harsh, whining noises. Charles was bent over it, his face flushed and perspiring, a streak of grease on his forehead. 'I can't understand what's wrong,' he muttered. 'Pass me that can of oil, Sara, please.'

Feeling utterly helpless, she watched him tinker with the rusty old motor, willing him to hurry—she must be there when David got home. However, the sun sank inexorably closer to the horizon; a chill wind sprang up, whitecaps dotting the channel that separated them from the land.

Charles finally straightened with a disgusted grimace. 'I think I've found the trouble, but it's getting too dark to mend it now. And of course, it didn't occur to me to bring the torch out of the car. Damn it, Sara, I'm sorry.' Wearily he wiped his face with a dirty rag. 'Still, the old fisherman told me there were oars, we'll row to shore now, while there's enough light left.'

But although they searched the grimy craft from stem to stern, there was no sign of the oars.

'One of the basic rules of boating is never to travel without them,' Charles berated himself gloomily. 'We'll just have to stay until tomorrow morning. Once it's daylight I'm sure I can get the blasted thing moving; we'd need light to negotiate the rocks, anyway.' He looked remorsefully at the girl's worried face. 'David will understand. I'll explain to him that it was completely my fault, and that I was the one who persuaded you to come in the first place.'

She tried to smile, but she was filled with a nameless apprehension. The tie between her and David was too new, too fragile. He would be home by now, wondering where she was. All Marilyn and Harold could tell him would be that she'd gone for a picnic with Charles; she hadn't told them she'd be back early for David. Hopelessly, she recalled David's antagonism every time Charles had casually flirted with her. And now she would be gone all night with him! What could be worse? For Charles's sake, though, she'd better try not to worry, and be a little more cheerful. So she said in a practical tone, 'I'm glad I brought my warm clothes, I'll need them. At least there's no sign of rain.'

Charles gave her a brotherly hug. 'That's my girl! I'll spread the tarpaulin between those two rocks, they'll shelter us from the breeze.'

Because his manner was so calm and matter-of-fact, Sara felt no embarrassment as she lay on the rather mildewed canvas, and he covered her with an old car rug. 'Sleep tight and don't fret—everything will be all right. I'm just going to have a last cigarette.'

Surprisingly, Sara did sleep, although she woke before dawn chilled and cramped, yet comfortable to hear Charles's even breathing beside her in the lonely darkness. The wind sighed in the branches; night creatures rustled mysteriously in the undergrowth. In spite of herself, images of David plagued her tired mind. If only she hadn't gone with Charles. . .if only David could have been delayed overnight in the city. She remembered his quick temper and furious face on their first meeting, and her spirit quailed. Dozing fitfully, she was awoken in the early dawn by the smooth rhythm of the motor. Her mood lightened, and she was able to wave jauntily at

Charles as she got up and stretched, sore in every limb. Oh, for a hot bath! Instead, she splashed cold brook water on her face and vainly tried to comb out her hair with her fingers—it was just as well she didn't have a mirror!

The boat carried them smoothly across the channel, as though determined to apologise for its previous reluctance, and it was only six-thirty when they reached the Rutherfords' house. Charles spoke softly. 'I'll go to my room by the side door so I won't disturb anyone. We'd better get a bit of sleep. I promise to see David later on today to make my apologies, OK?' He lifted her chin with one finger. 'Don't worry, Sara. And thank you for being so patient with me. I'm sure most other women would have been heaping coals of fire on my head by now. You're an angel.' He put his arm around her and kissed her lightly on the cheek, before disappearing into the house.

With mixed feelings, Sara took her damp swimsuit and towel out of the car. She ought to go to bed, it would be the sensible thing to do. However, she was certain she couldn't sleep. If only she could see David now, and straighten things out. . .

Her wish was granted with startling promptness, for David stepped out of the trees by the driveway and strode purposefully towards her. His body towered over her; cold fury masked his features. 'You finally decided to come home, did you?' he demanded, his words low and rasping with rage.

She leaned against the side of the car for support, her knees trembling. 'David, I'm so sorry,' she faltered, 'But I can explain everything.'

'Oh, I'm sure you can. You've had all night to think of convincing excuses, haven't you, you and Charles?' He laughed caustically. 'And to think I was foolish enough to say I could trust you—I even thought I loved you. In fact, I'd planned to ask you to marry me.'

She flinched at the raw contempt in his voice. 'I had a narrow escape, didn't I, Sara? You're just like the rest of them.'

Infuriated by her white-faced silence, he roughly plucked a fragment of spruce bough from her tangled hair. 'Where the devil did you spend the night? By the look of you, it certainly wasn't a hotel. Didn't he think enough of you for that?'

His ruthless taunts finally penetrated her frozen calm, stinging her to a heady, reckless anger. 'No, it wasn't a hotel. It was a beach on an island ten miles up the coast. But you wouldn't believe me if I told you we couldn't get home, would you? No, you believe the worst of everyone. Well, believe the worst then—Charles and I spent the night together. It's none of your damn business what I do, anyway. And I wouldn't marry you if you were the last man on earth!'

She faced him defiantly, taut with emotion, her eyes burning with unshed tears, a pulse hammering in the hollow of her throat. Fire leaped into his ice-blue eyes. He reached forward and seized her slim body in a cruelly strong grip. Although she struggled frenziedly, she was powerless to free herself, and he claimed her lips in a harsh and bruising kiss, that was utterly devoid of tenderness or love. She felt as though her heart would break when he thrust her violently from him, his chest heaving, his fists clenched by his side. 'I wish Charles joy of you!' he snarled, turned on his heels and was gone.

Near collapse, her limbs shaking uncontrollably, Sara fled to the sanctuary of her room and flung herself across the bed. But the long-awaited tears would not flow, even though her throat was tight with pain and her head pounding. For nearly an hour she lay there, heartsick and forlorn. Then the first sounds of the household stirring pierced her misery, and reluctantly she came back to life. David could trust a woman if he tried, she pondered bitterly. But he hadn't given her the slightest chance to explain, she had been condemned before she could even defend herself. Her pride, that most lonely of emotions, stiffened within her. If she had to bear this desolation, she would do it alone. She couldn't endure the sympathy Marilyn and Harold would offer if they were to know of her unhappiness.

Resolutely she got up and looked at herself in the mirror. Fortunately, a vestige of her sense of humour came to her rescue as she surveyed her bedraggled hair, crumpled clothes, and wan face. I'll have to do better than that, if I'm to convince them I'm heartwhole and fancy-free, she thought ironically. So she showered, washed her hair, dressed in a becoming shirt and slacks, and skilfully applied make-up to hide her pallor and the dark shadows under her eyes. Chin well up, she entered the kitchen, and was amazed to hear her voice say lightly, 'Good morning for the second time, Charles. Have you been regaling Marilyn with the tale of our expedition? I hope you weren't worried about us, Marilyn?'

'Well, I hate to admit it, but I didn't even know you hadn't come home,' Marilyn said. 'David got back around eight-thirty; he didn't say too much, but I got the impression he was disappointed you weren't here. I didn't know what time you'd be back, so I wasn't much help. He stayed until nearly midnight—I thought he'd never go home, I was having a hard time staying awake. After he went, we left the outside light on for you and went to bed.'

'Not much of a chaperon, is she?' Charles grinned. 'At least I haven't ruined your reputation.'

Sara turned away abruptly; through a haze of tears, she

busied herself pouring a cup of coffee. Her reputation was ruined all right, with the only person who mattered. Why, oh, why hadn't she mentioned to Marilyn yesterday that she'd be back in time for David's return? Perhaps then he would have assumed something had gone awry, instead of jumping to all the wrong conclusions.

Marilyn left the room, and Charles grabbed his opportunity. 'Shall I run over to David's this morning and make my explanations?'

'No, please don't bother, Charles,' she replied, outwardly casual, but inwardly bothered that she should have to deceive him. 'I'm sure I'll see him some time today, and I can apologise then. But thanks for the offer. May I have a piece of toast?'

If Charles was puzzled by her firm refusal, he was too polite to ask why she had changed her mind, and possibly sensed that she didn't want to discuss it further. 'What are your plans for the day?' he queried tactfully.

She followed his lead with gratitude. 'I think I'll take the children to Trout Brook. There's a swimming hole there, and they can fish too.' Unbidden, there flashed across her mind the memory of an earlier fishing trip, of a man's companionship, of a loon's wild cry. How could she stand these constant reminders of happier days? Even the prosaic little pot of wild strawberry jam on the kitchen table recalled the wonder of that early morning in the field with David. Luckily her innate courage came to her rescue; when Stephen burst into the kitchen, she diverted her thoughts and the day slipped easily into its soothing routine.

She was thankful for the children's company many times during the next few days. If she tended to keep them exceptionally busy, they didn't seem to mind. She stayed completely out of sight whenever David brought

Tim over, postponing the inevitable meeting with him. More than once, she caught Tim's blue eyes resting on her, and wondered if he suspected what had happened. She longed to ask him about his uncle, but forcefully stifled her questions. She must try and forget David, try and pretend that he didn't exist, and that he had never awoken this deep, abiding and painful love in her heart. Sitting on the beach one day watching the children play, she realised it was August already. School would open in September, the Rutherfords would return to Montreal, Tim and David to Rochford, and she, Sara, would be alone once again. Tears pricked her eyes. She blinked them away as Tim ran up the beach and dropped on the sand beside her.

To her consternation, he demanded without preamble, 'Did you and Uncle have an argument, Sara?'

She hesitated—what could she tell him but the truth? 'Yes, we did, Tim. Why do you ask?'

The little boy wrinkled his nose endearingly. 'He's as cross as a bear. I said something about you, and he told me he didn't want to hear about it.' His voice quivered. 'I wish you hadn't had a fight. Can't you make up?'

'Oh, Tim,' she sighed, 'it's not as simple as that. Grown-ups can't always forget their disagreements as easily as children can. Sometimes I wish they could.' She smiled at his sober face. 'Come on, let's take our buckets and hunt for crabs.' As they poked among the rocks and seaweed, she knew it wouldn't only be David she would miss; she was distressingly fond of Tim, longing to fill the gap his dead mother had left.

The dreaded confrontation with David took place the next day. Tim, Sara and the entire Rutherford family were lazily lying about the lawn after lunch, the children waiting impatiently until they could swim. Marilyn and Harold were discussing their proposed barbecue, when two cars came down the driveway: Dr Callaghan's bright red sports model spun to a halt in the gravel, and Sara's heart skipped a beat as David's car pulled up behind. She started to get up, frantically searching for an excuse to go in the house, but she was too late—the doctor hailed her loudly.

'Sara, I've been wanting to see you. Hi there, Tim, my lad,' and he rumpled the boy's hair. Regretfully, he declined Marilyn's offer of a beer. 'On duty, I'm afraid. Some iced tea would hit the spot, though. And where have you been hiding yourself lately, my dear?' he teased Sara.

Conscious of David's cold blue eyes studiously avoiding her, she stammered, 'Oh, I've been busy with the children, you know.'

'Well, I have a job to offer you,' Dr Callaghan swept on breezily, his shrewd eyes noticing the strain on her face, and wondering at its cause.

'That's not fair,' Charles protested. 'Here I am, trying to persuade her that Toronto is the ideal city for physiotherapists.'

Sara's breath caught in her throat as David directed a murderous look at Charles. Why couldn't Charles be quiet?

Seemingly impervious to this byplay, the doctor continued, 'I also want to have a look at this young fellow's leg. Let's go inside for a minute, Tim. Sara and David, will you come too, please?'

David held the door open for them. Sara brushed past him, her thick lashes lowered, miserably aware of the closeness of his body. She stood quietly while the older man checked Tim's leg thoroughly, then pronounced himself well satisfied.

'You did an excellent job, Sara. He's back to normal and in great shape. Off you go, Tim.' He glanced at

David under his bushy eyebrows. 'You have a lot to thank this young lady for. Tim wouldn't have recovered nearly as rapidly going back and forth to Saraguay for treatments.'

'I realise that,' David answered stiffly.

His grudging acknowledgement left a strained silence, and Sara said hurriedly, 'I was glad to do it.' There was an edge of defiance in her words as she added, 'I'm very fond of Tim.'

David's lips tightened ominously, and it was Dr Callaghan who filled the breach. 'Seriously, Sara, there's a position open for you at the hospital any time after the first of September. I'm sure we can reach an agreement about salary and living quarters. Or was Charles right— are you considering Toronto? There's no doubt you'd get a job there, particularly considering your experience in Montreal.'

She cast the doctor a look of entreaty. How could she tell him in front of David that she had no desire to go to Toronto, and that the little country hospital appealed deeply to her? How could she explain her worry that if she were to stay here, she would be unable to cope with the constant reminders of an unhappy summer love affair?

Breaking the tension, David stood up abruptly. 'I'm certainly not needed to help you sort out Sara's future. Maybe Charles should be included to plead his case. Good afternoon, Dr Callaghan, and thank you.'

With a curt nod he was gone, his sarcasm lingering behind him. Sara's knees gave away beneath her, and she buried her head in her arms, a wave of grief overwhelming her.

'So that's the way of it,' mused the doctor. 'I'm a blind old coot not to have seen it before. You picked a difficult one to fall in love with, girl. That fiancée of his did a real piece of work on him. Now she was a female I couldn't take at all. Listen, my dear, we'll forget about the job for a while, it's there for you and you have a month yet to make up your mind.' He patted her roughly on the shoulder. 'Try not to take it too much to heart. Maybe you'd be better off going to Toronto. Charles seems pleasant enough, and there are definitely more diversions there than here.'

Sara smiled up at him mistily, grateful for his clumsy attempts to comfort her, causing Dr Callaghan to add gruffly, 'David must be daft, a beautiful girl like you. Any sense in me having a word with him?'

'Oh, no, please don't!' Sara exclaimed in horror. 'That would be dreadful. I feel better already, just having shared it with you. I'm sure I'm not the first woman to love the wrong man, and I don't suppose I'll be the last.' But this bleak philosophy seemed cold comfort as the summer days slowly passed.

CHAPTER EIGHT

ABOUT a week later, Sara awoke one morning with no presentiment that this day would be different from any other. She coped easily with the children, ignoring the dull ache that was continually with her since the estrangement from David, insensibly soothed by the regular routine of trips to the beach, picnics and walks with Lady and Benedict. As she sat with Harold and Marilyn on the veranda that evening, she wondered whether they noticed how rare David's visits had become. Perhaps he was using his writing as an excuse to cover his absence. It was fortunate they never asked, she thought.

She felt no warning premonition that evening when the phone bell shrilled in the house, shattering the quiet dusk.

Harold got to his feet. 'I'll answer it, it's probably the long-distance call I'm expecting from Montreal.' He disappeared, and they could hear him talking in the living room. 'Hello. Yes, speaking. . .'

There was a pause, and the listeners noticed the blank astonishment in his voice as he continued, 'Linda. . . Linda Barrett? Well, well, it's been a long time! You'll have to forgive me for not recognising your voice. Where are you?. . . You're only a couple of miles away then. Do you have a car?. . . Sure, Marilyn would love to see you again. Come and have a drink with us now. We'll expect you in half an hour. . . Fine, we can catch up on the news when you get here. Goodbye, Linda.'

A cold fist clenched Sara's heart—surely it couldn't be

David's ex-fiancée, she prayed, as Harold returned to the veranda, his face wreathed in a genial smile.

'You'll never guess who that was, honey,' he said to his wife. 'Linda Barrett. She's staying at the Mariner Lodge for a few days and would like to come and see us.' He turned to Sara. 'Linda was once engaged to David—a charming girl, I'm so glad she phoned.'

If Marilyn's response was rather lukewarm, her husband's enthusiasm compensated for it; Sara remembered Marilyn's earlier admission that Linda was one of the few people about whom she and Harold had disagreed. Conscious only of a wild desire to flee, she finished her coffee in two quick gulps. 'I'll get the children bathed and settled in bed for you, Marilyn,' she offered. 'You'll want to be here when your guest comes.'

Marilyn grimaced, wrinkling her upturned nose. 'I'd better be, I guess. Thanks, Sara. Join us as soon as you're finished, won't you? Charles should be home a bit later too, he's having dinner with a business friend.'

'I ought to write letters,' Sara pleaded weakly, and quickly escaped to the playroom. The rough and tumble of bathtime restored her equanimity, and when she curled up at the foot of Patricia's bed to read to them she was touched as always by their scrubbed cleanliness and damply curling hair.

They were all three deeply engrossed in the troubles of Winnie-the-Pooh when Marilyn spoke from the doorway. 'Oh, there you are, Sara. I'd like you to meet a friend of ours from Ottawa, Miss Linda Barrett. Linda, this is Sara Haydon, who's been such a wonderful help with the children this summer.'

Sara blushed at Marilyn's praise, unconsciously looking very young as she sat cross-legged on the bed in her faded jeans, her hair pulled back in a ponytail, a streak of bath powder on her cheek. 'How do you do, Miss

Barrett?' she said politely, and received a cool nod of condescension from the slender blonde, whose polished sophistication made her spirits sink. Linda's make-up was flawless, subtly emphasising her violet eyes and pouting lips. Her simple beige shantung dress must have been a Paris original, a string of perfectly matched pearls encircled her throat, and a huge diamond ring sparkled and glittered on her finger.

'We'll see you a little later, then,' Marilyn reiterated. Indignantly, Sara tried to ignore Linda's slightly raised eyebrows as this invitation was issued; for the first time in the Rutherford's house, she had been made to feel like hired help, and it was a most unpleasant sensation.

After she had tucked the children in, she went to her room, where she thoughtfully surveyed her wardrobe. In the end, she chose the very becoming pale yellow shirtwaist she had worn for her birthday, and she took particular care with her hair and make-up, while a spray of Charles's perfume further raised her morale. She was walking down the hallway when she heard Charles himself whistling tunelessly in the kitchen.

'You're looking extremely elegant,' he exclaimed, and offered her his arm with a mock bow. 'Do allow me to escort you!'

So it was that she entered the lounge with her arm in Charles's, laughter lighting up her fragile loveliness. Linda's eyes narrowed in sudden calculation.

Harold informally introduced the younger man. 'My brother, Charles, Linda, Miss Linda Barrett, Charles.'

Linda radiated charm as she held out a gracefully-shaped hand to Charles, who debonairly bent over it, rather spoiling the effect by flashing a surreptitious wink at Sara as he straightened. 'Very pleased to meet you, Miss Barrett. Are you on holiday in the area?'

'Yes, I'm at the Mariner. I haven't really decided how

long I'll stay yet. And please, call me Linda.' She smiled archly at the smitten Harold. 'I'm renewing old acquaintances whom I've neglected rather badly. I can't believe how much the children have grown since I saw them last, Marilyn. How pleasant for you to have help with them. Miss Haydon, are you enjoying your summer here?'

'Yes, thank you, I am indeed. They're three delightful children.' Too late, Sara realised her mistake.

'Three?' Linda repeated. 'But you don't have a third, do you, Marilyn?'

'Sara's referring to Tim Ramsay, David's nephew; he's over here more than he's home, I think, and Sara kindly includes him in her outings with my two.'

'You must have your hands full, unless he's improved considerably,' Linda intervened, an unwonted sharpness marring her pretty voice. 'I found him a most difficult little boy, and perpetually dirty.' Fastidiously, her fingers smoothed the immaculate fabric of her dress.

Exasperation made Sara forget her nervousness. 'I can't agree with you, Miss Barrett. Tim's an engaging child and very well-mannered, although a trifle over-imaginative at times. And any normal child should have a healthy layer of dirt by the end of the day.'

Linda smiled unpleasantly. 'Of course, you're being paid to remove it, aren't you, Miss Haydon? Perhaps you look at it a little differently from the way I do.' She turned to Marilyn, artfully shifting her body in an endeavour to exclude Sara from the conversation. 'How is David these days? I suppose he's married with a young family of his own now?'

'Oh, no,' Marilyn retaliated, running her hands through her red curls, a spark of anger in her green eyes. 'David's been wary of the female sex since you left, Linda. I'm afraid he's a confirmed bachelor. He's been working quite hard this summer, he always seems to have his nose buried in a book.'

'He always did work too hard,' Linda languidly replied. 'But I'm sure I can persuade him to leave those dusty old tomes of his for a few days; all work and no play, you know.'

Her cool air of confidence that David would drop everything at her whim nettled Sara, but her voice was deceptively calm when she spoke. 'He wouldn't be the head of his department at the university if he didn't work hard, would he, Miss Barrett? And besides, he loves his work and derives great satisfaction from it.'

Mutual animosity flared in grey and violet eyes; Charles, amused at this byplay, hastened to create a diversion. 'I'm sure I've seen you somewhere before, Linda. I wonder if it was at Senator MacQuarrie's cocktail party in May—I was in Ottawa right after my return from Europe. Weren't you there with Fraser Ryan, the young Liberal Member of Parliament?'

His tactics were successful; Linda smiled reminiscently, fluttering her long lashes with devastating effect. 'Yes, I was. Such a charming and talented man. Do you know him, Charles?'

The conversation became general, so that Sara's ruffled feathers subsided somewhat, enabling her to study Linda dispassionately. Oh, heavens, she was beautiful! No wonder David had been head over heels in love with her—and perhaps still was. But, David, her intuition cried, she's all wrong for you! She'd like you to be a useless playboy, a mere appendage of her wealth and glamour. And she hates children, you don't need much insight to see that. Still, how could any man resist such a combination of charm, money, and dazzling good looks? Look at Charles and Harold, both hanging on to her every word!

As though aware of her unspoken criticism, Charles

flashed her a conspiratorial grin. 'We've been discussing Toronto, Sara. Have you applied for a job there yet? Linda, I'm trying to persuade her that Toronto is the heart of Canada, so she'll come to work there. There's an excellent hospital three blocks from my office, come to think of it.'

'You're a nurse, are you, Miss Haydon?' Linda questioned.

'No, a physiotherapist.'

'Head of the children's department at her last job in Montreal,' Harold put in, not letting Sara get away with this modest answer.

Patently unimpressed, Linda said coolly, 'I must have you look at my left knee, it's been weak since I strained a ligament last summer, playing tennis. It could do with some massage, I expect.' She seductively crossed her silken-clad legs, drawing attention to her delicate ankles and tiny feet in handmade shoes.

Sara's hackles rose again. What an insufferable creature! She, Sara, was undoubtedly supposed to be delighted to have the privilege of massaging Miss Linda Barrett's knee! She'd see about that. Fuming inside, she left her seat and joined Marilyn, who was making fresh coffee in the kitchen. She relieved her feelings banging the fragile Wedgwood cups and saucers on the tray, until her sense of humour reappeared, luckily before any damage was done. She made an expressive face at Marilyn. 'Sorry, your guest and I seem to disagree on every subject that comes up.'

The redhead giggled and whispered, 'I can't stand the woman. My darling husband thinks she's marvellous, and laps up every word she says. Let's produce the coffee and hope she won't stay much longer!' More seriously, she added, 'I wish there was some way I could warn David she's here.'

But the next day, Sara was to wonder if 'warn' had been the right word as far as David was concerned. Tim had come over after lunch, quiet and subdued, pushing away Benedict's advances with uncharacteristic irritation. Worried about him, Sara murmured, 'Is something wrong, Tim?'

He lifted his small face, and the girl was shocked by the gleam of tears in his blue eyes. 'Miss Barrett's come back,' he burst out. 'She was kissing Uncle David, then she sent me over here so they could talk. And Uncle David had promised to take me bird-watching today. I just hate her!'

Alarmed, Sara knelt in front of him, speaking slowly as she searched for the right words. 'I don't think she understands small boys very well, Tim dear,' she said. 'She doesn't realise you like to explore the woods, and climb over rocks and get grubby playing. I guess you'll have to be extra patient if you can. I know it's not easy. Perhaps your uncle forgot about his promise, it's quite a while since he saw Linda, so I expect he was excited.' A mental picture of Linda in David's embrace passed painfully across her vision, but she pushed it aside grimly and added, 'Come on, cheer up, chum. I thought we'd weed the vegetable garden this afternoon, as it rained last night. Afterwards, we can have a swim at the cove to clean up. How does that sound?'

A smile wavered on his lips. 'OK. I'll try to be patient, like you said.'

Understanding only too well how he felt, Sara devoted the next hour to keeping all three children in fits of laughter at her jokes and riddles, as they worked their way down the neat rows of carrots, spinach, beans and peas.

'Hurray, we've finished,' Stephen announced proudly. 'It didn't seem to take very long. Look, here comes

Uncle David. Who's that with him?'

'That's Miss Barrett,' Tim said dolefully.

Sara straightened to see the couple sauntering towards them, Linda's hand resting confidingly on David's arm, her feet daintily picking their way down the uneven path. She looked exquisitely cool in a pale halter dress, frivolous sandals of the same shade, a lacy and unquestionably expensive sunhat shading her flawless complexion.

Sara stifled a sigh as she contrasted her own attire—muddy rubber boots, brief red shorts and sleeveless gingham blouse, gardening gloves coated with earth, the whole outfit topped by an old straw hat of Harold's.

Linda's laugh rippled sweetly in the warm air. 'How ambitious you are, Miss Haydon! I wish I had your energy in this heat. Goodness, look at the mud on you, Timothy! Run to the house and make yourself presentable quickly. We're going to visit friends at the hotel where I'm staying.'

'But we're going swimming,' Tim started to protest.

'Don't argue so,' Linda scolded, but doggedly Tim persevered.

'You were supposed to take me bird-watching today, Uncle David—you promised!'

David's mouth hardened. 'We'll go another day. Now do as Linda says, and tidy yourself up. You could do with a clean shirt, too.'

The boy's eyes sought Sara's morosely, as though to say, I told you what she's like.

Trying to project encouragement in her tone, Sara said quietly, 'Off you go, love. Better brush your hair while you're at it.'

A forlorn figure, he trudged up the path. Linda said caustically, 'Really, is all this messing about in the garden necessary? Surely Harold could hire a competent gardener to look after such things.'

'I do consider it necessary, Miss Barrett,' Sara answered, keeping a tight rein on her wayward temper. 'I think children need some idea of responsibility as they grow up. The three of them have to weed and water the vegetable garden all summer; and each one has other small chores they do through the week.' She smiled, trying hard to be friendly. 'The mud washes off, but I hope the sense of responsibility stays with them.'

A flash of pure venom crossed the blonde girl's perfect features. 'You're quite the child psychologist, aren't you? You should be married with a half a dozen of your own.' She ran her fingers lightly up David's bare forearm. 'Come along, darling, or we'll be late. I don't want to keep the Warrens waiting.' Without even a glance at Sara, David turned towards the house, helping Linda over the rough ground as if she were a fragile piece of china, his head lowered to her uplifted face.

Sara was dismayed to feel hot tears flood her eyes. So this was how jealousy felt, this burning pain in body and soul. 'Oh, damn,' she muttered wearily. 'Damn, damn, damn. Why on earth did she have to come?' She slowly gathered the garden tools and replaced them in the shed, deliberately delaying until the roar of a car engine signalled that David, Linda and the reluctant Tim had gone.

Her depression was deepened the following day, a day as hot and sultry as the previous one. By early evening, a light breeze had sprung up; restlessly, Sara decided to walk to the little handicraft shop half a mile along the road, Patricia contentedly accompanying her. Possibly she could find something there for Joan's birthday. But somehow the contents of the shop seemed a bit homespun for the sophisticated Joan, so Sara settled for handcarved wooden Indians for the boys, and a knitted doll's dress for Patricia's Miss Moppet.

They left the shop hand in hand, Patricia carefully clutching the parcel, her small face wreathed in smiles. She enjoyed having Sara to herself once in a while. Consequently, it was to please Sara that she waved vigorously at the sleek green Jaguar speeding towards them. 'That's Miss Barrett,' she exclaimed. 'Stephen says it's a terrific car, he'd like to have a ride in it.'

To Sara's consternation, the Jaguar purred to a stop beside them. Linda was driving, David sitting close to her, his arm draped in a proprietorial manner across the back of the seat behind her. 'Can I give you a lift?' the blonde enquired demurely.

Sara was about to refuse, but was forestalled by Patricia, who jumped up and down, her voice a squeak of delight. 'Yes, please. I'll be able to tell Stephen I had a ride in the Jaguar!'

Linda looked taken aback by this ardent response, so Sara explained as she climbed in the back seat, 'Your car has caused great excitement with Stephen, and I'm afraid he'll be green with envy to think his sister has driven in it. Just drop us at the end of the driveway, Miss Barrett. I don't want to take you out of your way.'

'We have to pick up Tim anyway. I wish he were as anxious as Stephen to ride with us, don't you, David darling?'

David gave a non-committal grunt. For a moment, Sara allowed her gaze to dwell lovingly on his tanned neck, and tousled hair, which the sun had bleached to the colour of ripe wheat. In less than a month he would return to the university, out of her life. It would be unendurable...even the torture of seeing him in Linda's company was better than not seeing him at all.

However, there was no sign of her inner turmoil as she politely thanked Linda for the lift; she held her head high with unconscious dignity during the seemingly endless walk to the house. Pride was a tremendous help at times, she thought, with a wry grin at herself, and I'll need every bit of it to get through the rest of this month. But her composure faltered when she bumped into Charles in the Hallway.

'What's the joke, honey?' he asked. His smile faded, for her lower lip was quivering uncontrollably; instinctively he folded her in a warm embrace. 'Come on, tell Uncle Charles what's wrong. That blonde iceberg getting to you? I can't say I blame you. Honestly, Sara, I don't see how David can be in love with her. She's as phoney as a three-dollar bill,' he concluded slangily. He felt her slender form relax in his arms, and gently rubbed his cheek against her glossy hair. 'Mmm, you smell nice. Listen, I was hoping to talk to you anyway. Marilyn and Harold want to take the children to White Point tomorrow, so why don't you make it your day off? We can laze around the beach in the morning, then go into Saraguay later on for dinner, and evening at the theatre. There's an Ontario company here on tour, and Harold mentioned he had a couple of tickets they wouldn't be using. It would do you good to get away from it all. Besides, there's nothing I'd like better than a whole day of your company. How does it sound?'

'Charles, you're a dear,' Sara murmured, her voice muffled in his shirt front. 'I'd love to go, and I promise not to weep all over you.' She gave him a watery smile in the dusk, and it took considerable restraint on his part to release her and say lightly, 'It's a date. I'll get on the phone to book a table for dinner.' He disappeared into the kitchen, whistling jauntily.

Thank you, Charles, she thought silently, you came to my rescue just when I needed you. It was tempting to encourage his affection, for it was a balm to her wounded heart. But in all honesty, she knew that was all it was; Charles's embrace had comforted her, but David's had set her blood singing in her veins, her heart pounding in her breast. Two men, one whom she loved, one who apparently loved her. . .she would forget it all tomorrow, and simply relax and enjoy Charles's company. She could at least do that much for him.

And she found it an easy task. The day dawned clear and fresh; however, feeling deliciously indolent, Sara buried her head under the covers, shutting out the riot of bird song, and went back to sleep.

An hour later, Mrs Donnelly tapped on her door. 'Are you awake, Sara?' She emerged rosy-cheeked and dishevelled, to hear the housekeeper cluck indulgently, 'Breakfast in bed this morning. Young Mr Rutherford said to spoil you today, and indeed it's high time for that.'

'Thank you, Mrs D. That looks really appetising—I'll bring you the tray when I've finished. What a beautiful day!'

'Take your time, dearie. Mr Charles is on the veranda whenever you're ready.'

The door closed softly behind her, and Sara attacked the scrambled eggs and toast with gusto. Afterwards, she slipped into her bikini and beach coat, pulling her hair on to the top of her head with a ribbon and letting it tumble down in loose curls. Charles was lying on a lounge chair in the sun, clad in sea-green swimming trunks, his tanned body lithe and muscular. He opened one eye when she approached.

'Hello, honey. It's too warm for anything energetic this morning, isn't it?'

'You're bone lazy!' she laughed. 'But as it happens, I feel exactly the same way. Maybe we can bestir ourselves to swim before lunch, do you think?'

The hours idled by, and in the late afternoon as Sara showered the salt water from her skin and hair, she felt a small urge of hope—she could enjoy herself without David. She had refused to think about him all day; if treacherous memories had assaulted her, she had pushed them away—it was an art she would have to improve upon in the future. . .

Charles's appreciative reaction to her bright cotton dress was all she could have wished; she had sewn it in a low-backed style, with a full-length slim skirt, slit up to the knee, and she carried a light stole draped over her shoulders. He enlivened the long drive to the city with a description of some of his business associates, amusing her with caustic and often libellous sketches of prominent politicians and businessmen.

The scenery unfolded in breathtaking magnificence; as they rounded a bend in the road, Sara interrupted him. 'Just look at that shoreline, Charles—pure white surf, azure waves, dark green hills, granite cliffs. No wonder I love this country! And where else but in Canada would you drive two hundred miles for an evening at the theatre? Naturally I'd like to go back to England for a holiday, who wouldn't? But I think I'd find it too crowded to live there now. Big cities aren't my thing—although I'm certainly looking forward to this evening. Typical contradictory female, I'm afraid!'

The play was a sparkling and hilarious comedy, exactly what Sara needed, and she was still chuckling when they came out of the theatre to the darkened street. 'I'm weak from laughing so much,' she confessed.

'Would you like a coffee before we go home?'

Sara tilted her head to one side. 'Do you know what I'd really like? A French pastry with lashings of whipped cream! I can work it off tomorrow with the children!'

'That's easily enough satisfied, honey.' They walked

down the empty pavement arm in arm, and entered the deserted foyer of a French restaurant. Charles leaned forward to remove Sara's stole, his hands brushing her bare shoulders, and impulsively she said, 'Thank you, Charles, for taking care of me so well today. I have enjoyed myself.'

Her grey eyes gazed candidly up at him, and his brown eyes warmed. Lowering his head, he kissed her softly on the lips; in gratitude she responded, so that their bodies merged into one silhouette. The restaurant door opened, and they moved apart guiltily, to hear an only too familiar voice.

'Dear me, how very public! Is that a Montreal custom, Miss Haydon?'

A flush suffused Sara's cheeks, for it was Linda with David, a Linda obviouslsy bent on cheapening Charles's gesture.

But Charles refused to be intimidated, replying debonairly, 'A kiss for a beautiful girl who has given me a day to remember, Linda. How are you, David? Why don't you join us? Sara is going to gorge herself on French pastries, but I think I'll stick with coffee.'

His smooth good manners gave Sara the time she needed to collect herself. Her eyes had flown to David's craggy face like a magnet, and had surprised on it a rush of pure rage that puzzled her. Why should he care if she kissed Charles? Could it be that his feeling for her was not as dead as he would have her believe? Her confused thoughts were interrupted by Linda's petulant refusal. 'We wouldn't want to intrude, would we, David darling?'

'You won't be intruding,' Charles insisted, leading them to a table. 'Please sit down. We've just come from the theatre, a very funny play.' He shot a teasing glance at his companion. 'Sara laughed so hard she's hungry again. After the dinner we had, honey, how do you keep your sylph-like figure?'

Linda superciliously ignored their casual banter; she was exquisitely gowned in mauve chiffon, her sleek blonde hair elaborately coiffed. Diamonds adorned her ears and fingers, their cold gleam reflected in her violet eyes. 'Well, you've had a busy day, haven't you?' she snapped. 'Quite an outing for you, Sara.'

Irritation flared in Sara's breast. She treats me as though I were the scullerymaid, she mused resentfully. But Charles came to her defence again, challenging David with his direct gaze.

'I think it's high time somebody waited on Sara; she's far too good-natured, you know. By the time she's looked after everyone else and their children, she doesn't have much time left for herself.'

'We all know what a paragon of virtue Sara is,' Linda acknowledged sweetly, managing to turn the compliment into a subtle insult.

'Oh, Linda, be quiet,' David ordered. 'Charles is right. We do take advantage of her.' His granite features softened, reminding Sara of the cliffs' rugged outlines blurred by the sun. 'And we only have to ask Tim to get a list of her saintly qualities!'

For the first time in many long days, his gaze met Sara's in guarded friendliness. Sudden joy made her speechless, but her happy face was answer enough: for a brief moment, they could have been alone in the room.

The spell was broken when the waiter brought coffee and a tray laden with delicious pastries. Even though the incident was not repeated, David relapsing into his former cool politeness, its magic remained with Sara on the long journey home, armouring her against the lonely days that followed. Tim was spending more and more time at the Rutherfords', and although Sara knew it was because he was avoiding Linda's continual presence at David's, not even this knowledge could entirely quench the little spark of happiness.

CHAPTER NINE

THE postmistress, that fund of local information, had told the Rutherfords about the influenza that was racing through the village children. Even so, Sara was completely unprepared when the phone rang the following evening. It was nearly eleven, and she and Mrs Donnelly had been chatting over a cup of tea in the kitchen: Charles, Marilyn and Harold were attending a convention dinner and dance. Mrs Donnelly picked up the receiver. 'It's for you, dear,' she said, passing it to Sara.

Mildly surprised, Sara said, 'Hello,' and sat down abruptly as she heard David's deep voice on the line.

'Sara? It's David.' There was a perceptible pause, which she was quite incapable of filling. 'I have to ask a favour of you. Tim has the 'flu; Dr Callaghan was here an hour ago and left some medicine, and the sickness simply has to run its course. But he's feverish, he won't sleep, and he keeps asking for you. I've told him you'd come in the morning, but he wants you now.' He continued with an obvious effort, 'Linda tried to help, but she only made matters worse, so I sent her back to the hotel. Please will you come?'

Without stopping to think, she answered, 'Of course I will. I can take Marilyn's little car, so I'll be there in a few minutes.'

'I'll go and tell him you're on your way, then. Thank you, Sara. Goodbye.'

She hung up, hurriedly explaining the situation to the housekeeper. 'I don't know when I'll be back, but tell Marilyn not to worry.' She threw her suede jacket around her shoulders, for the summer evenings were chilly, and ran out to the car, anxiety for Tim flooding her mind – she was aware that David wouldn't have phoned if he hadn't been desperate. Swinging down his drive, she parked under the tall pine tree by his garage. In spite of her worry, she could not control the hammering of her heart against her ribs as she rang the bell, distastefully eyeing the insects circling around the outdoor light.

David opened the door, and in the split second before he spoke, seemed to absorb every detail of her appearance: bare feet thrust into thonged sandals, slim-fitting denim jeans, scoop-necked pink T-shirt, dark hair swinging loosely about her face. Her eyes looked black in the lamplight and were filled with apprehension. 'Come in, Sara,' he said harshly, his face severe and unreadable. 'I can't do anything with him. The doctor said the medicine wouldn't take effect immediately, and I'm afraid he was right.'

He preceded her to Tim's room; she halted in the doorway, absently handing him her jacket, a tiny sound of compassion escaping her as she saw the little boy's hectically flushed cheeks and restless movements. She walked quietly over to the bed. 'Tim,' she said, 'it's me, Sara.'

His eyes flickered open, fastening on her with difficulty. He grabbed her hand with burning fingers. 'Don't go away. I'm so hot,' he muttered fretfully.

'No, of course I won't.' Thankful for her hospital training, she deftly made his bed more comfortable.

David re-entered the room, looking tired and harassed. 'Can I do anything?'

'Yes, please,' she replied, adopting a briskly business-like manner to banish the constraint between them. 'A clean pillowcase and fresh pyjamas, and a bowl of cool water. We'll see if we can get his temperature down a bit.'

The 'we' slipped out so naturally that she didn't notice it, and together they bathed Tim's fevered limbs, and changed his sweat-soaked pyjamas. Because Sara's presence seemed to soothe him, she was careful not to leave the vicinity of the bed. While David propped Tim up in his arms, she encouraged the boy to sip some fruit juice; his uncle's gentleness as he lowered the small body back on the pillow touched her heart-strings. What a wonderful father he would make—which, of course, was absolutely none of her business. . .

Tim seemed a little quieter, so she whispered, 'Why don't you have a rest, David? I think he's over the worst, but if I need you for anything, I'll call you.' Was it her imagination, or was he relieved to leave her?

'Perhaps I will—be sure to call, won't you?'

An hour later, Tim's fever mounted suddenly; Sara bathed him again, and it was nearly two in the morning before he quietened. Wearily she pulled an armchair beside the bed and curled up in it, a blanket over her knees. Tim's fingers clenched trustingly in hers. In spite of herself, her eyelids drooped and closed, and her breathing became slow and rhythmic in sleep.

The house was still for over an hour—it was when the mahogany grandfather clock chimed three that David woke with a guilty start, upbraiding himself for falling asleep. He went down the silent hall to Tim's room, and in the dim light of the bedlamp, he could see his nephew slumbering peacefully, his face no longer pink with fever. Sara's body had twisted uncomfortably in the chair, and the blanket had fallen to the floor. Carefully the man detached her hand from Tim's; bending over, he picked her up. Her head fell back across his arm, baring the graceful line of her throat; her long lashes made dark smudges against her skin. His grip tightened unconsciously, and her eyes fluttered open. 'David?' she murmured drowsily.

'Hush, everything's all right. Go back to sleep.' With a childlike sigh she nestled in his arms, and he carried her to the spare bedroom, laying her on the bed and removing her sandals. He pulled a quilt over her recumbent body, hesitated a moment, then leaned over and brushed her cheek with his lips. She stirred in her sleep; for several minutes he remained watching, his features inscrutable in the darkness, before soundlessly returning to the vigil by Tim's bed.

Bright sunlight was streaming in the window when Sara opened her eyes, momentarily confused by the unfamiliar room. Where was she? Then recollection poured back of David's appeal for help and the anxious hours spent with Tim. She must be in the spare bedroom; with growing consternation, she noticed her sandals placed neatly by the bed and the quilt that covered her. David must have put her here—she had a dreamlike remembrance of strong arms encircling her, of a fleeting touch of lips, and a wave of shyness overwhelmed her. And look at the time—it was nine-thirty! She'd slept for hours.

She tiptoed to the bathroom, where she did the best she could to make herself presentable, then crept into Tim's room. He was sleeping tranquilly, his forehead cool. Poor little boy, he had been miserable.

She hesitated in the hall, surprised to recognise Marilyn's voice talking to David in the kitchen, and increasingly relcutant to face him. But she needn't have worried; her friend's presence bridged the awkward moment, although she did wonder if David's eyes lingered on her flushed cheeks.

'Marilyn brought us homemade muffins and strawberry jam for breakfast,' he said matter-of-factly. 'I'll pour your coffee.'

He pulled out a chair for her, and she wished him a

rather timid and abashed good morning. 'I had no idea it was so late.'

Marilyn smiled. 'From what David tells me, you deserved your sleep. I'm so glad Tim's feeling better.'

'I'm the one who should be feeling guilty,' David apologised, passing her the cream and sugar. 'Sara sent me off for a rest about midnight, Marilyn, and I went out like a light. I wasn't much help, I'm afraid.'

Before the girl could think of a coherent reply, the phone rang in the other room; she gathered her wits enough to ask Marilyn if she had enjoyed the dance. When David came back a few minutes later, there was a dazed expression on his face, and he said grimly, 'It never rains but it pours—there's a lot of truth in these old clichés. That was a colleague of mine; the chap who was supposed to teach the second session of the summer school in English literature has just had an operation, and I'm the only one who can replace him at such short notice. They want me there tomorrow if I can possibly make it.' He ran his fingers through his hair in exasperation. 'The joys of being a department head!'

Sara gripped her coffee cup in both hands to hide their trembling, while cold dismay enveloped her. Tomorrow he would be gone...

Marilyn's practical voice penetrated her distress. 'That's a shame, you'll miss the barbecue we're having before Charles goes. But what about Tim, David? You can't take him with you now, he's not well enough to travel. You'd better leave him with us, we can drop him off in Rochford at the end of the month.'

'That's a very generous offer, but I can't take advantage of you like that.'

The redhead intervened tartly, 'Now, David, you know perfectly well he's with us most of the time anyway. Linda's not a bit good for him, you surely realise that.'

Her candour made the man wince, and lines of strain furrowed his face. 'Yes, you're right, I'm sorry to say. It's a problem. . .'

Sara's fingers tightened around her cup. It could only be a problem if he planned to make his relationship with Linda permanent; otherwise, why would it matter what Tim thought? Through a haze of dejection she heard David's formal thanks for her help, his mind evidently already occupied with plans for his unexpected departure—with chilling certainty, she was sure he had forgotten her, pushed her aside for more important considerations. Numbly she said goodbye, and Marilyn affected not to notice her stricken looks.

She did not see him again before he left, intentionally avoiding him when he brought his nephew over; the boy was wrapped in blankets but well on the way to recovery, and in tearing spirits at the thought of a fortnight at the Rutherfords'. Sara was frightened that her composure would shatter under the strain of another farewell, so she pleaded a headache, that was not altogether theoretical, and stayed in her room. Through the open window she could hear David's familiar deep voice speaking to the Rutherfords, then the car door slammed and he was gone. She fell across the bed and wept disconsolately, muffling her sobs in the pillow. David, David, I love you so much. . .

Fortunately, Marilyn had arranged the barbecue for the next weekend, and she deliberately involved Sara in as many of the preparations as she could; she knew hard work alone was no cure for a broken heart, but at least it would keep Sara from brooding, and Marilyn's unspoken sympathy was a comfort to the younger girl.

When Saturday dawned bright with sunshine, Marilyn heaved a sigh of relief, confessing that rain would have ruined all her plans. As the guests started to assemble,

TO TRUST MY LOVE 133

late in the afternoon, long tables had been set under the trees, laden with a variety of salads, homemade rolls and relishes. Lawn chairs dotted the grass, while Harold and Charles had the coals hot in the barbecue pits; Benedict and Lady were in close attendance, wistfully eyeing the heaped platters of beef. Friends gathered in groups, chatting over cocktails and admiring the panoramic view of woods, sand and surf; the air filled with the tantalizing aroma of charcoal-grilled steak.

Sara decided it was a pleasant and informal way of entertaining, and for the first time since David's departure, felt slightly hungry. Dr Callaghan sat down beside her, threw her a breezy compliment, and with a characteristic lack of finesse demanded, 'What about the job, young lady? Are you interested?'

She took a deep breath—she had to settle her future sooner or later. 'I've been thinking about it and, yes, I would like to work for you.' Oh dear, how excited she would have been in the spring at the thought of a job in a small country hospital on the edge of the wilderness! But since meeting David, her priorities had changed, and the prospect no longer thrilled her. However, she had to have a job, and perhaps in the back of her mind was the memory of David's statement that he frequently came up here in the winter.

Dr Callaghan was so genuinely delighted that she felt ashamed of her lack of enthusiasm. 'I'll drop in some forms for you to sign on Monday while I'm on my house calls. You'll have to make up your mind where you're going to live, too; there are a couple of rooms in the back wing of the hospital, or I know of a small house for rent nearby, it's clean and in good condition.'

'I'd prefer the house,' she said, trying to infuse some eagerness into her decision. 'I'm quite used to being on my own. Probably I could have a look at it within the next couple of days, and let you know.'

A hand fell on her shoulder, and she smiled up at Charles; his other hand was supporting a plate shamelessly laden with steak and salads. 'Have to keep my strength up,' he joked, then challenged the doctor with mock ferocity, 'I hope you're telling her all the advantages of working in Toronto, but judging by your self-satisfied air, I expect I'm wrong!'

The older man retorted, 'Meet the newest member of my staff. You'll just have to open a branch of your insurance company in Terence Harbour!'

Charles grimaced. 'Not much hope of that.' His brown eyes met Sara's apologetic ones, and he said reassuringly, 'Don't look so worried, honey.'

With unusual tact, the doctor disappeared in the direction of the food, and Charles gently covered her hand with one of his. 'I didn't really think you'd come to Toronto, Sara. I know how you feel about David, and I can understand why you'd prefer to stay around here.' He grinned crookedly. 'I'll be back next summer, and if by some miracle you're still unattached, I'll try again. How's that?'

She was profoundly relieved by his ready acceptance of her plans, sensing intuitively that Charles had by no means been as deeply involved with her as she had been with David. And with a pang, for the first time she noticed Linda; she was talking to the local game wardens, her petite seductiveness very much in evidence as the two burly men hovered over her. How long would Linda stay at the Cape now that David had gone, for surely he had been the main attraction? Sara could not have foreseen how soon and how unpleasantly she was to find out.

As darkness descended, the trees were charmingly lit with miniature Chinese lanterns, giving a fairy-tale and romantic air to the scene, that filled Sara with an ache of loneliness. Searching for distraction, she carried a trayload of used glasses up to the deserted house, where she pushed open the kitchen door with her elbow, glad to be alone for a while. A sudden noise from behind startled her, and she whirled in fright. A glass flew off the edge of the tray; in horrified fascination she watched its contents cascade down the side of Linda's tailored trousers.

Frowing in vexation, the blonde cried spitefully, 'You little fool! Look what you've done!'

'I'm so sorry, Miss Barrett,' Sara stammered, recoiling from Linda's animosity. 'I didn't know anyone was here. Please let me wipe it off, then perhaps it won't show.' She knelt, managing to sponge away the worst of the stain, and said repentantly, 'You must allow me to pay for the dry-cleaning.'

'That won't be necessary. I'm leaving in the morning, to stay with friends in Rochford. Naturally David's expecting me to join him there. I imagine our engagement will be announced very shortly.'

The colour drained from Sara's face; she leaned against the table to support her shaking limbs.

Linda's violet eyes narrowed speculatively and she taunted, 'Why, I do believe you thought David was attracted to you—what a ridiculous notion! David doesn't say much about it, but he's an extremely rich man, and moves in the best social and intellectual circles. He would hardly interest himself in you. He and I have many mutual acquaintances and it will be a most suitable match. After all, why do you think I came here this summer?' She laughed scornfully. 'Certainly not to see the Rutherfords, or to enjoy the rustic pleasures of Rocky Cape. Frankly they leave me cold. But I'd heard David was still a bachelor and I was quite confident I could get him to propose. He always was like putty in my hands.

The only fly in the ointment is Tim—David's besotted with the boy. I shall have to hire an elderly housekeeper so we can be independent and travel whenever we like.'

Sara stood as though turned to stone, and Linda shrugged irritably. 'I was crazy to let him go three years ago, I was too young to realise what a rarity a man like him is—brains, breeding, and that rugged masculinity make a powerful combination. I get tired of fortune-hunters. David certainly doesn't need my money, he has plenty of his own.' An unkind smile flitted across her perfect features. 'Well, Sara, won't you congratulate me?'

Her grey eyes oddly compassionate, Sara said soberly, 'I wish you the happiness you deserve. Goodbye, Miss Barrett.'

The summer days fled past, and for once Sara was glad to see them go: the Cape was a different place without David and Charles. Since the disastrous interview with Linda, she had accepted the inevitability of a marriage between the vindictive blonde and her beloved David, and her lacerated feelings had mercifully sunk into a blessed numbness. Unfortunately, Tim still had the power to hurt her; the children were making the most of their remaining days of freedom, Tim apparently as carefree as his two companions. Sara's heart ached for him as she thought of his bleak future, abandoned by David and Linda to the 'elderly housekeeper'. But she was helpless to intervene, so she fiercely concentrated on her own prospects which were falling slowly into place.

She had inspected the house suggested by Dr Callaghan, and had been pleased with its fresh-painted charm and spotless cleanliness. It was a tiny bungalow, built in a grove of poplars and birches within sight of the sea. She arranged for some of Uncle Matthew's furniture to be taken out of storage and delivered by moving van, and ordered material for curtains. She had been completely taken aback when Marilyn and Harold insisted she have the use of Marilyn's car for the winter.

'Much better for it to be driven regularly than to sit in the garage until next summer,' Harold said briskly, waving away her objections. 'You certainly can't depend on our famous bus to get you around, so no more arguments, miss!'

Sara's emotions were alarmingly close to the surface these days, and she had to blink away tears when she spoke. 'Thank you both so much. Not just for the car, although that will be a marvellous help, but for everything all summer. You're the nicest couple I've ever met, I'm going to miss you.'

'We've loved having you,' Marilyn assured her. 'I'm afraid Stephen and Patricia can't understand why we're not taking you to Montreal with us. You've become part of our family.'

She paused and Harold took over. 'We'll be sending you an airline ticket some time in November for a flight to Montreal—we'd like you to spend Christmas with us; it always seems to arrive before we know it, and we wanted to invite you in person.'

Sara accepted, genuinely pleased, and with this invitation in mind the last few days were much less difficult. She helped Marilyn pack, took the children on farewell expeditions to their favourite haunts, and finally gathered together her own clothes and books. As she took down the painting David had given her, in that faraway happy time when she had been sure he was beginning to love her, she was disturbed by a light tap on the door, and saw Tim's head peering around it. 'Hello, Tim, come in.'

He smiled at her, unusually shy, and confided, 'I came to say goodbye now, I didn't want to wait until tomorrow when Stephen and Patricia would be there.'

Touched, she said, 'We've had a good summer, haven't we, Tim? But you'll be glad to get back to school and see all your friends again, won't you?'

'I guess so,' he agreed, apparently absorbed in pulling a piece of fluff from his sleeve. Then he added in a rush, 'Will Miss Barrett still be going around with Uncle David?'

Her heart sank, but she managed to say reassuringly, 'I don't really know. You'll just have to trust your uncle—I'm sure he'll do whatever's best for you.' But will he? she wondered silently. If he's in love with Linda, will he consider Tim's feelings?

'I wish he'd marry you instead,' Tim burst out unhappily. 'I like you much better.'

'Thank you, dear, that's a lovely compliment. But you can't arrange grown-ups' lives for them, Tim. Perhaps your uncle will let you visit me in my new house—would you like to do that?'

This idea cheered him up considerably, and after he had gone, Sara sank on the bed with a sigh of relief—she'd been afraid there would be tears.

The sky was overcast and a steady rain was falling the next morning. Harold carried Sara's belongings out to the little car, and loaded his own station wagon. Goodbyes were of necessity a bit hurried, to avoid getting soaked to the skin. Sara went up the driveway ahead of the Rutherfords, and as she turned to the right and then to the left, the children waved frantically, shouting, 'We'll see you at Christmas! Goodbye, goodbye!'

She waved back, then resolutely pulled away. A summer came to an end.

CHAPTER TEN

SARA kept herself busy at the bungalow for the rest of the week, rearranging Uncle Matthew's furniture, and lovingly polishing the well-worn surfaces, as she whiled away the hours with memories of the years they had spent together. After she had sewn curtains, and bought kitchen utensils and bed linen, the little house began to seem like home. With stubborn courage, she hung David's painting prominently in the living room—she had that memento of him, if nothing else.

Her new job started on the Monday morning, and rapidly absorbed a great deal of her time and energy. Until midday, she worked in the hospital with the patients there. However, in the afternoons, she made house calls, many to older people unable to make the journey to the Harbour for treatments, for she covered a territory of some fifty miles, up and down the meandering coastal road.

Very soon, she came to know and respect the gnarled and weather-beaten fishermen and their families. Their lives were physically strenuous and often dangerous, but they had a simplicity and unpretentious kindness that many a city dweller might have envied.

Except for one, thought Sara unhappily, as once again she drove past the dreary shack, its yard littered with rubbish. Oh, dear, it was still there. 'It' was a starved and miserable-looking Alsatian, chained to a dilapidated kennel behind the dwelling. Why did people keep an animal if they couldn't look after it? She wanted to get herself a dog for company, but when she had thought of it earlier, she had pictured a clean and fluffy pup, fat and healthy. A far cry from that mangy and pathetic creature! Still, perhaps she would go and see the owners; after all, she wouldn't have to commit herself—she would do it at the end of the week.

So on Friday afternoon, she parked the car beside the tumbledown house, walked towards the kennel, then stopped and clucked gently, holding out her hand. The dog regarded her with sad brown eyes. He cautiously sniffed her fingers, his tail gave a feeble wag, and Sara was lost.

She had no trouble persuading the slatternly housewife to accept her money; with a distinct feeling of triumph, she detached the chain and coaxed the dog to the car. What a good thing she had bought a dish and some tinned dog food, just in case. And some flea powder, she ruefully congratulated herself, as the dog began to scratch itself vigorously. 'I shall call you Prince,' she told him firmly, 'because in a very short time, I'll have you looking like a prince.'

Indeed, within a fortnight, he was no longer recognisable as the scruffy beast she had brought home. There was a spring in his step, his coat was starting to shine, and, far more important, his initial wariness was slowly giving way to a fierce affection—he followed Sara everywhere and greeted her after work with wild enthusiasm. He developed a deep-throated and very reassuring bark, and no longer did she feel nervous alone in the bungalow at night.

Therefore, it was Prince who gave warning of a completely unexpected visitor a few days later. Sara was rinsing out a uniform in the sink when he started to bark. Surprised, she wondered who it could be—it was nearly nine o'clock and pitch dark. She opened the door, then stared in blank amazement. 'Why, Tim! What on earth are you doing here?'

The boy stood on the step, a small suitcase clutched in one hand. His face was tired and grimy, his eyes uncertain of his welcome.

'Come in, dear. It's all right, the dog won't hurt you. Get down, Prince! Tim's a friend. Are you by yourself?'

She ushered him in and closed the door behind him, regarding him steadily. 'Something's wrong. Tell me about it.'

He finally found his tongue. 'I ran away, Sara,' he gulped. 'I didn't know where else to go, so I came to you. Linda says Uncle David is going to marry her—she doesn't want me around, that's why I decided to come up here and see if I could live with you.'

She interrupted him. 'But doesn't your uncle know where you are?' He shook his head miserably. 'Oh, Tim, he'll be terribly worried. When did you leave?' His white-faced fatigue made her suddenly break off her inquisition, saying instead, 'You look dirty and hungry. You can have a quick bath while I cook some supper for you, and then we'll talk. Off you hop, the bathroom is the second door on the right. There are lots of towels in the cupboard.'

She walked back to the tiny kitchen, her mind whirling with conflicting thoughts. So Linda and David were to be married. . .and Tim had run away rather than face living with them. She jumped as the phone rang, and said absently, 'Hello.'

'Sara? It's David Ramsay. I'm sorry to bother you, but I'm worried about Tim. In fact, I'm just about ready to call the police. He left as usual this morning, but apparently he didn't go to school, and he hasn't come home since. I suppose you haven't heard from him, by any chance?'

Too perturbed to be tactful, she answered baldly, 'He's here.'

There was a charged silence before his voice crackled along the line, vibrant with anger. 'I suppose this was arranged between the two of you, was it? When were you planning to let me know his whereabouts? Bring him to the phone—I want to speak to him.'

Her fingers clenched convulsively around the receiver; however, there was no trace of fear in her even reply. 'No, you can't speak to him, David. Contrary to your belief, I had no idea he was coming. He arrived about ten minutes ago, he's worn out and needs something to eat and a good night's sleep. Quite apart from that, he's obviously a very unhappy little boy. I would suggest you come up here to see him, and I would also suggest you leave that foul temper of yours at home. It's the last thing he needs now.'

Appalled by her own temerity, she waited for a scathing rebuff, but after a long pause, David merely said, 'I see. I imagine the problem is Linda, am I right?'

Unable to be anything but completely honest, however much it would hurt him, she said soberly, 'Yes, I'm afraid so.'

There was another silence before he spoke. 'Very well, I'll come as early as I can tomorrow. Goodbye.' With a decisive click, the connection was cut.

Prince pushed a cold nose into her hand, and she expelled her pent-up breath. 'Phew! Prince, how do I get in these messes? I'll never know. . .well, I'd better feed Tim and stop worrying about it.'

The youngster shone with cleanliness when he reappeared in his pyjamas. Tentatively, he made friendly advances to Prince. 'He's a nice dog. When did you get him?'

'I bought him nearly three weeks ago,' she explained.

'But as you can see, he's already made himself very much at home. Come and eat, Tim, I think everything's ready.'

As he ate the bacon and eggs, she took the opportunity to study him covertly. His face was thinner and paler than it should be; there were shadows under his eyes. She made sure he had eaten his fill, then suggested, 'Why don't you tell me what's been upsetting you, Tim? Your uncle phoned while you were in the bath, and he's coming tomorrow.'

'I bet he's cross,' Tim lamented. 'But I couldn't help coming. Miss Barrett has been in Rochford since Uncle David started the summer school. She's staying with friends, but she's at our house most of the time. And she's always going somewhere with Uncle David, I never see him any more. He hasn't even set up my electric train again, he hasn't had time.' He continued defiantly, 'She says I'm to call her Aunt Linda, but I won't. She wants to send me to a boarding school so I'll be out of the way. I do try to behave when I'm with her, but it never seems to work out, and she's always angry about something I've done. So couldn't I live with you, and go to school here, when they get married?'

The hope in his vulnerable little face died away at her serious reply. 'I don't expect so, Tim. It's not as simple as that. Don't fret, though. When your uncle comes tomorrow, I'll talk to him, and explain how you feel— we'll just have to see what he says.' She smiled. 'You're asleep on your feet, chum. I'll show you to your room. You've my very first visitor, do you realise that?'

She tucked him into the spare bed, and drew the curtains. 'Sleep tight, Tim. You can take Prince for a walk in the morning, if you'd like to. He loves to go back in the woods and chase the squirrels.' She kissed him and put out the light.

Her face abstracted, she made a cup of coffee and

curled up in the armchair to drink it. She could already feel her nerves quiver at the thought of the forthcoming interview with David. She had been hurt when he had immediately jumped to the conclusion that she and Tim had planned today's escapade. He didn't trust me that night with Charles, and he hasn't trusted me since, she mused unhappily. He'll never let Tim stay here; his answer will be the same as Linda's—an elderly housekeeper, some cheerless old lady who's forgotten what it's like to be young.

For a long time, she sat there staring into space, her coffee growing cold, as she relived the events of the past summer. Ever since she had been a teenager, she had been confident that some day she would meet one certain man, the only man who would fulfil all her expectations, and with whom she would fall deeply in love. But in her dreams that love had always been shared, a reciprocal current of feeling between two people completely committed to each other. She had never visualised that she would love a man who seemed almost to despise her, who perpetually suspected her of the worst. When she finally went to bed, she tossed and turned restlessly, and her sleep was fitful, punctuated by nightmares.

For Tim's sake, she made an effort to be cheerful as she prepared breakfast, and showed him how to feed Prince. 'I'm still giving him two meals a day, until he fills out a bit more,' she said, passing the dog food. 'He was skin and bones when I got him.'

Tim volunteered to wash up, while Sara quickly dusted and tidied the little house. Then she dressed in a becoming pair of green and beige checked trousers and a tailored beige blouse, brushing her dark hair until it shone. She had calculated that David couldn't arrive before noon, so she pulled on her suede jacket and offered to show Tim the path through the woods where she took Prince for his walks.

They stepped outside into a perfect September morning, with just a slight chill in the crystal clear air. Golden rod and Michaelmas daisies rampaged through the ditches and dotted the hillside with yellow and purple; a few maples were aflame with scarlet. The leaves of the delicate poplars trembled and rustled in a vagrant breeze. In the distance, they could hear the irregular hammering of a woodpecker.

'What a gorgeous day!' Sara exclaimed. 'Look, the path goes between those two spruces. If we're lucky, we might see a deer, I've often seen tracks in the mud.'

They walked slowly towards the forest, Prince gambolling ahead to examine all the fascinating scents in the long grass. They were almost hidden by the trees when Sara heard the purr of an approaching motor. Her stomach tightened with apprehension as a car pulled in by the bungalow and its door slammed. Her eyes met Tim's in a moment of mutual appeal. 'Chin up,' she said softly.

They emerged from the dark shadows of the spruces into the clearing, and she called, 'We're up here, David!'

Prince bounded down the hill to meet the intruder, and Sara couldn't help feeling amused at the ease with which David made friends with the unruly animal. And even under these circumstances, how heavenly it was to see him again! As they approached, he straightened, tall and handsome in twill trousers and a turquoise heavy-knit sweater, a silk scarf tucked in the neckline; his eyes were disturbingly blue in his tanned face.

'This is a new acquisition, isn't it?' he said, scratching Prince between the ears while the dog stood in silent ecstasy, plumed tail waving.

'Yes, I haven't had him long. He's good company in the evenings,' she replied, then could have bitten off her tongue at this admission that she might be lonely.

He glanced keenly at her, but all he said was, 'An Alsatian usually makes a good watchdog. You're wise to have him.'

He turned his attention to Tim, who was standing warily beside Sara, obviously not knowing quite what punishment to expect. The man knelt, and clasped his nephew's shoulders in his strong hands, the two fair heads level with each other. 'You gave me a rough time yesterday, young fellow,' he began. 'But all the same, I think I owe you an apology. It was as much my fault as yours; I've been neglecting you lately, and I'm sorry. But that's over now—Miss Barrett has gone back to Ottawa today, and things will get back to normal again.'

Tim blurted out in complete surprise, 'Aren't you going to marry her?'

David's features tightened grimly. 'No, I'm not. Grown-ups make mistakes sometimes too, Tim.'

Tim could no longer hide his elation as he asked eagerly, 'Will you set up my train?'

'Yes,' his uncle laughed. 'I promise to do it as soon as we get home. Now why don't you take the dog for a walk? I want to talk to Sara.'

'Sure. Come on, Prince.' And the two of them pranced exuberantly up the hill, leaving Sara to wrestle frantically with the implications of David's speech. She had anticipated having to defend Tim from his uncle's wrath—instead, David had admitted that he himself had been in error, and had apologised with a straightforward honesty for which she respected him. But what had it cost him to give up Linda? She remembered his grim demeanour and was certain he could not have done it easily.

She dragged her attention from the two retreating figures, and reluctantly met David's serious eyes. He was leaning against a silver birch tree, sunlight dappling his lean body, his untidy hair ruffled by the breeze. She lowered her thick lashes before his penetrating gaze, a warm blush flooding her cheeks.

'Look at me, Sara,' he insisted. 'I have something I want to ask you.' Unwilling she obeyed. 'That's better. Don't look so frightened, I'm not going to eat you. I'm sorry for the suggestion I made on the phone that you had encouraged Tim to run away, I know there was no truth in it. I was so worried, I didn't know whether I was coming or going. For several weeks I've been avoiding a situation that's gone from bad to worse—I knew Linda was a bad influence on Tim, perhaps I kept hoping things would improve. Well, yesterday showed me they wouldn't, so, as you heard me tell Tim, Linda has gone.'

He fell silent, as though recalling that farewell, then continued bleakly, 'As you probably know, I was appointed Tim's guardian when his parents were killed, and at the time I swore I'd always try and do what was best for him. I've done a lot of thinking since yesterday, and it all comes down to this—you're the only woman I know who can provide the love and care Tim needs. So will you marry me, Sara?'

The colour drained from her shocked face. Whatever she had expected, it had not been a proposal of marriage. And what a businesslike proposal it was! Tim might need her love, but David was making it painfully clear that he himself didn't want it. Unconsciously, she shuddered and moved a step away from him, her hand held up as though to ward him off.

The sun was in her eyes, so she didn't see him flinch at her gesture, as if she had struck him. His eyes narrowed to ice-blue slits. His voice harsh, he persevered doggedly, 'I had hoped the idea wouldn't be altogether repugnant to you. I want you to understand that Tim would be your only responsibility; I would make no demands on you, and you would be my wife in name only.'

Anguish filled Sara's breast as his meaning penetrated her distress. In her imagination, how many times had she pictured the moment when David would ask her to marry him, and as she joyfully accepted, would enfold her in the shelter of his arms? How different was the actuality! Naturally, convention wouldn't allow her to be his housekeeper; to have her for Tim, he was forced to marry her. Her heart cried out for one word of love, even a single touch of affection. But as she saw his tight-lipped disdain, she shivered—her wish was in vain. He loved Linda, but his sense of responsibility to his dead brother's child would not allow him to marry her.

He demanded abruptly, 'I take it you refuse?'

'Oh, David,' she faltered, 'I don't know what to say. I can't answer you now, you'll have to give me time to think.' Her voice trailed off miserably, and he shrugged.

'The only persuasion I can use is that Tim badly needs you—you realise that as well as I do, Sara. The two of you get along like a house on fire, I've watched you on and off all summer.'

Again she made that tiny motion of protest; with a grunt of frustration, he halted. In the distance they heard Prince bark, and Tim's answering shrill whistle. With a visible effort, David forced himself to speak quietly. 'Look,' he offered, 'let's put all this on the shelf for a while—I can see I've taken you by surprise. I booked into the hotel at the Harbour for the night, I don't have to go home until tomorrow afternoon. Maybe you can let me know by then what you decide, or if not, in a few days' time. Meanwhile, let's do our best to give Tim a good weekend, shall we? I need to make amends to him. It's warm enough for a picnic, we could go down to the shore somewhere. Would you do that for me?'

His unlooked-for kindness brought a rush of tears to

Sara's eyes; she swallowed and answered huskily, 'All right. It's a good idea. I'll make some sandwiches.'

From the privacy of the kitchen window, she saw David stride through the trees to meet Tim, swinging the boy high in the air while the dog barked hysterically at his feet. How could she accept his offer? It would be a marriage based on falsehood from the beginning. Yet loving him as she did, which was worse—an artificial marriage or a complete separation? For if she refused, she was certain she would never see either of them again: David would make sure of that. There would be only a blank and empty future before her. . .

Sternly, she took herself to task; David had told her to put it on the shelf, and it was advice worth taking. She would forget the difficult decision ahead of her, accepting the unexpected gift of an afternoon with him. She found it pleasant to forgo her independence, to allow him to help her into the car and carry the picnic basket for her. He made no demands on her, treating her with an impersonal courtesy and friendliness that was soothing to her jangled nerves. Perhaps, she thought doubtfully, he was trying to show her that a relationship such as he had suggested was possible. Certainly Tim was delighted with their company, and his high spirits smoothed over any awkward moments they might have had.

She enjoyed taking them to the breakwater at Terence Harbour and introducing them to some of the fishermen there, whose speculative looks at her handsome escort she firmly ignored. One old man, a former patient, presented them with lobsters, fresh from the sea. 'Enough there for you and your man and the little fellow,' he said with a sly wink, chuckling wickedly at Sara's rosy cheeks.

She felt a surge of pride in her companion: he might be a social and intellectual catch in Rochford, as Linda had claimed, but he was also perfectly at ease, joking with the homely fishermen on the wharf. They cooked the lobsters for supper, eating the succulent flesh warm from the shell. By nightfall, Tim was asleep on his feet, so Sara hustled him into the bath, paying no attention to his half-hearted protests.

'We had fun today,' he said drowsily, after Sara and David had each kissed him good night. With a contented sigh, he buried his head in the pillow, and Sara was warmed by a glow of achievement. How much better he looked now than when he had arrived, so woebegone and bedraggled! Maybe David's idea wasn't so crazy after all.

He helped her clear up the kitchen, tactfully not pressing her for an answer, and soon afterwards took his leave. 'I didn't get much sleep last night. I'll come and get you both for lunch tomorrow; there's a small dining-room at the hotel. Sleep well, Sara. Whatever you decide, today was a good day.'

She closed the door softly behind him, a tide of exhaustion washing over her. Everything could wait until tomorrow...

She awoke early from a deep and refreshing sleep; in the clear morning light, the situation seemed much simpler. She would marry David, for with her usual honesty she knew she didn't have the courage to deny him. And who knew, perhaps in time she could exorcise the ghost of Linda's presence. But until that time she was determined not to reveal her true feelings; she would hide behind a manner as cool and detached as David's own.

Fortunately, when he arrived, Tim was off somewhere with Prince, so she could at least greet him alone. Outwardly composed, it took every ounce of her pride to say steadily, 'I accept your proposal, David. I'm sure Tim will benefit from it, and you are aware how fond I am of him.'

For a full minute he stood motionless, his hands thrust deep in his trouser pockets, surveying the cold dignity on the girl's features. She felt her knees begin to shake and forced herself to remain calm. His tone was aloof when he finally spoke. 'I see. Well, I'll make some arrangements when I get home. How about two weeks from now?'

She fought back a panic-stricken impulse to turn and flee. It was one thing to marry David at some indefinite date in the future, quite another to have the time narrowed down to a mere fortnight. 'I don't think it could be quite that soon,' she gulped. 'I'd like to give Dr Callaghan a month's notice, he's been so kind to me.'

'Cold feet already, Sara?'

She flushed with annoynace at his unkind reproach. 'Not at all. I've said I'll marry you, and so I will.'

'Let's settle on the last week in October, then. That should appease your conscience sufficiently. I expect you'd prefer a register office to a church wedding?'

'Hmm, you're probably right. We might as well put the best face we can on the whole thing.' Although his sarcasm made her flinch, he paid no heed. 'It happens an old school friend of mine is the vicar of a small church in Rochford. I'm sure he'd be delighted to perform the ceremony for us. I should think the best thing for me to do is reserve a flight to Rochford next weekend for you, you could come Friday evening and leave late on Sunday. I know my mother will be anxious to meet you. I must get in touch with Marilyn and Harold, too.'

Her eyes widened in dismay—she'd forgotten about his mother. She conjured up a mental picture of a formidable grey-haired dowager, and again had to conquer the urge to flee. It was no comfort to hear David say airily, 'Don't look so worried. She'll love you. Here comes Tim; it's all right if I tell him the news?'

She nodded dumbly, her mind in a whirl, but dimly aware that once Tim was told, she could not possibly back out.

'Hi, Uncle David,' the little boy shouted. 'I found an old robin's nest with a broken egg in it, look!'

David grinned, no trace of his former disdain visible. 'We have a surprise for you—how would you like to go to a wedding next month?'

'A wedding? Whose?'

'Sara and I are going to be married. She'll be coming to live with us in Rochford.'

Tim looked from one to the other, while jubilation slowly dawned in his face. 'Are you really, Sara?'

His uncomplicated happiness resolved all her qualms; her smile was radiant. 'If it's all right with you?'

'Oh, yes, I think it would be great. Uncle David, if you're getting married, aren't you supposed to kiss her?'

'Well, yes,' David admitted mischievously, 'as a matter of fact, I am. I shouldn't think it would be a proper engagement otherwise, would you, Tim?'

Sara's face grew pink under their concerted scrutiny. 'That's not fair, you're ganging up on me,' she protested. As David's arms came around her and his mouth met hers, she held her body rigid to quell its trembling, and by a supreme effort, her lips were cool and unresponsive. Twin devils of anger danced in the man's blue eyes when he released her; however, Tim was obviously satisfied. Sara was thankful he didn't request a repeat performance when they left for Rochford that afternoon, the boy waving goodbye as the car disappeared round the bend.

She perched on a garden chair in the sun, suddenly overwhelmed by the enormity of what she had done. She'd agreed to marry a man who did not love her, who was using her for his own ends, a man, moreover, whom

TO TRUST MY LOVE

she was helpless to resist. In a month she would be Mrs David Ramsay, and Tim, to all intents and purposes, would be her son. . .

CHAPTER ELEVEN

SARA went to work the next day in fear and trembling, but, contrary to her expectations, Dr Callaghan didn't seem particularly surprised by her resignation, and she had to avoid his suspiciously shrewd eyes when he congratulated her. It was more difficult to parry the curious questions of other members of the staff, some of whom were frankly envious of her good fortune.

All too soon it was Friday. In a daze, she packed, took Prince to a neighbour, and drove to Saraguay. When she boarded the aircraft for the short flight to Rochford, she was too preoccupied to notice the appreciative male eyes following her progress. To bolster her faltering morale, she had put on the smartly tailored red coat that she had worn for the long-ago luncheon with Harold, the day it had all begun; she had intentionally done her hair in a more sophisticated style than usual, determined that David should not have to be ashamed of her.

The young man in the seat beside her tried to engage her in conversation; although her replies were abstracted, he gallantly carried her overnight case off the plane, and his face fell when she politely refused his dinner invitation. 'My fiancé's meeting me, I'm sorry.'

'Not my lucky day,' the young man said regretfully. 'But it was nice meeting you.' He tipped his hat and was lost in the crowd.

David, waiting behind the barrier, was a witness to the episode. When Sara greeted him with tremulous shyness, he took her case, saying brusquely, 'Who was that fellow?'

'I don't know,' she replied honestly, puzzled by his interest. 'He sat by me on the plane. I wasn't really paying much attention to him—I guess I'm rather nervous about meeting your mother.'

Apparently her explanation satisfied him, and while he skilfully wove in and out of the heavy traffic he pointed out local places of interest, pride in his voice when he showed her the gracious, ivy-clad buildings of the university where he taught. The car left the busy city streets behind, purring down avenues of discreetly elegant houses. Even so, Sara was totally unprepared for the impact David's home made on her.

They were driving past what she had assumed was a park, huge old trees and flowering shrubs behind a wrought iron fence. To her surprise, David passed through the iron gate posts into a narrow, tree-lined lane, which opened to a sloping expanse of manicured green lawns, shaded by magnificent oaks and beeches. The house was a rambling two-storeyed structure of mellow brick, its mullioned windows twinkling in the sunset. It had an air of dignified welcome; smoke rose lazily from one of its many chimneys. Behind it, Sara caught a glimpse of stables and a white-painted paddock. To the left, thick-growing pines sheltered an enormous swimming pool. A meticulously tended rose garden perfumed the evening air; clustered chrysanthemums rioted their autumnal colours on either side of the massive front door.

As David pulled to a stop, Sara faced him accusingly. 'Oh, David,' she wailed, 'you never told me you were rich. I wasn't expecting anything like this!'

To her consternation, he threw back his head and roared with laughter. 'Sara, you're priceless! Any other woman would be only too happy to find herself engaged to one of the wealthiest bachelors in the entire province.

You'd have something to complain about if I were taking you to starve in a garret!'

In spite of herself, the corner of her mouth tilted upwards. 'I suppose you're right. But you have to admit that driving me around the countryside at Rocky Cape in the old jeep, wearing that disgraceful jacket of yours, was hardly any preparation for this. Honestly, I had no idea...'

His humour was contagious, and when he guided her into the house, his hand under her elbow, they looked the image of a happy couple in complete accord. The elderly lady standing in one corner of the lounge nodded to herself in satisfaction, before moving into the glow of lamplight, her hand outstretched. 'You must be Sara,' she said warmly, noting with approval the girl's delicately chiselled features and candid grey eyes, widened in sudden nervousness. She kissed Sara on the cheek. 'I'm delighted you're here. David, you are to be congratulated on your choice.'

Sara felt as though a weight had been lifted from her shoulders—the formidable dragon of her nightmares faded away, never to return. Instead she saw a gracious woman in her early sixties, whose lined face and white hair spoke of the sorrows of her life, but whose eyes were the clear, friendly blue of delphiniums on a summer day.

Racing footsteps clattered down the curved staircase. Tim burst into the room and flung his arms around Sara's waist. She bent to hug him, and at the sight of their evident affection for each other Mrs Ramsay's last doubts were allayed. Tim dragged Sara away to see his electric train, and at his bedtime she read him an adventure story, serene in the confidence that David's mother liked her, and that the path she had chosen was the right one.

Later, when Mrs Ramsay showed her to her room, Sara exclaimed in delight at the soft green Chinese carpet, and gleaming mahogany furniture, although again the unobtrusive luxury slightly intimidated her. The older woman drew the heavy gold curtains. 'I hope you'll sleep well, my dear. Tomorrow I expect David will show you the house, and I'd like to take you in to Rochford, then we have a few people coming for dinner. I understand from David that you'd both prefer a small wedding?'

'Yes, we would. I don't have any relatives, and I think David only wants to invite his immediate family and some particularly close friends.'

'I see. I can probably make most of the arrangements for you then, as you have to work almost to the day. By the way, it did my heart good to see you with Tim, he's talked about nothing else all week. You're very much in love with my son, aren't you, Sara?'

Evasion was impossible with David's gentle mother. Sara heard herself say, 'Yes, I am.' She was too tired to control the quiver in her voice. 'But he doesn't love me, Mrs Ramsay. He loves Linda Barrett; I saw them together too much this summer to doubt that. He's marrying me because he thinks I'll make a good mother for Tim—he told me so. And I will,' she promised fiercely, tears feathering her lashes, for it was a profound relief to be able to reveal the tensions of the past few days.

'I'm never quite sure what's going on in David's mind,' his mother confessed. 'Certainly Linda made herself very available while she was here. I was terrified he'd marry her, she's such a cold-hearted and basically selfish person, but that beautiful exterior could turn any man's head, I suppose. I'm sure, Sara, that everything will work out for the best. I know you're exactly the kind of girl I've always wanted for my daughter-in-law.' She embraced Sara lightly and left the room, her lavender scent and comforting words remaining behind her.

On Saturday, David formally escorted his fiancée through his home, introducing her to the various members of the staff as they went from one beautifully appointed room to another. The girl was dazed by the procession of antique furniture, luxurious rugs and valuable paintings that passed before her eyes.

'My father built it to resemble an English country house,' David explained. 'He was born in Surrey, emigrated to Canada and made his fortune, but he always had a soft spot for the Old Country, as he called it. He had a lot of the furnishings imported after he settled here. He loved the garden; he transplanted honeysuckle, rhododendrons, daffodils and wallflowers. Some grew, some didn't—not even he could tell the Canadian climate what to do! I can remember him cursing the early frosts in September and the late ones in June, poor old Dad!'

She listened in a fascinated silence, eager for any details she could glean of his family life, but abruptly he changed the subject.

'There's Mother. I think she wants to take you shopping. Her idea of a wedding is a lot of new clothes and a long white dress.'

His cynicism shook her to the extent that when Mrs Ramsay said on their way to the city, 'You must let me start your trousseau, Sara,' she hesitated uncomfortably.

'I can't let you do that, Mrs Ramsay.'

'Please, dear. I never had a daughter, and I would truly enjoy it.' Sara found she didn't have the heart to refuse her charming hostess.

The next couple of hours passed in a whirl of lacy négligés, dainty slips and panties, and rainbow-hued skirts and sweaters of soft cashmere. Their final purchase was a dinner dress of deep blue velvet, a dress so beautiful it took Sara's breath away. Its lines were severely elegant, subtly enhancing the swell of her bosom and her tiny waist. She gazed entranced into the mirror; it would take a good part of her savings, but she longed to have it and adamantly insisted on paying for it herself.

'You could wear it this evening,' Mrs Ramsay suggested thoughtfully. If her son could resist Sara in that dress, he wasn't made of flesh and blood!

Sara couldn't suppress a tremor of pure excitement that evening as she descended the graceful stairway. In her impatience to put on the dress, she was ready rather early, so she made her way to the library—a pleasant, book-lined room with a cheery red shag carpet and a fire crackling in the brick hearth. She wandered slowly along the laden shelves, trying to come to grips with the incredible notion that in four short weeks she would be the mistress of this sumptuous house. How her father would have loved this room!

The door swung open; overcome with shyness, she saw it was David, unfamiliar in tailored evening clothes and immaculate white shirt, gold cuff links gleaming at his wrists. The formality of his attire only served to emphasise his height, broad shoulders, and strongly hewn features.

'Oh, there you are, Sara,' he said coolly. 'I was looking for you. I think it's about time we discussed engagement rings, don't you?'

His nonchalant attitude flicked her on the raw, for her vanity was wounded by his indifference to her appearance. 'I don't think there's anything to discuss, I can well do without one.'

'Come now, I've never known a female yet who could

resist the glitter of a diamond.'

'Well, you've met one now!' she retorted. 'Let's at least be honest with each other and admit this is no ordinary engagement.'

With an air of decision, he carefully closed the door behind him, and walked towards her, holding her mesmerised by the sudden fire in the blue depths of his eyes. 'When I see you looking as beautiful as you do now, I'm apt to forget it,' he challenged, and ran one finger slowly and deliberately down her neck and across the creamy skin of her bare shoulder.

Helpless to move, she shivered at the intensity of feeling roused by his touch. Unconsciously her eyes pleaded for him to stop.

Violently he pulled his hand away; his voice was suddenly weary. 'It's all right, Sara, you don't have to worry. I'll keep my part of the bargain. I told you it would be marriage in name only, and so it will.' Striving to introduce a lighter note, he continued, 'But on the subject of the ring—that gorgeous dress definitely requires some jewellery, so will this do?'

Bewildered, she watched him reach in his pocket and extract a small square jeweller's box. He flipped open the lid, and nestled in the black velvet was a ring that made Sara catch her breath in enchantment: it was a single large sapphire surrounded by a circle of sparkling diamonds.

'Hold out your hand,' he ordered, slipping it on her finger. 'Consider yourself officially engaged, Miss Haydon!'

Uncertainly, Sara looked up at him, for his harshly lined face belied his light words. 'It's a lovely ring, David. I wasn't expecting one at all, you know.'

'I'm glad you like it,' he said briskly. 'Certainly no one could accuse you of being mercenary, Sara. There's the doorbell, we'd better go and see who's arrived.'

As they entered the hall, Mrs Ramsay appeared, regal in black satin and diamonds, her hair a snow-white coronet about her head. The three of them stood beneath the glittering chandeliers, while Sara was introduced to a bewildering succession of David's friends: the men in full evening dress, their wives elegantly gowned, all frighteningly self-possessed. Their faces passed in a blur, and she despaired of remembering their names. As though David sensed her nervousness, he stayed close by her side when they moved into the drawing room for cocktails, deftly guiding the conversation for her, the epitome of a tenderly solicitous fiancé.

He beckoned to the vicar who was to marry them, a thin-faced scholarly man, with an unexpected twinkle in his eye. With the skill and sympathy inherent in his profession, he immediately set Sara at ease, and for the first time, her smile was relaxed and spontaneous. He drew her out little by little, and before long she was the centre of a small group, amazed to hear herself laughing and talking with complete composure.

A little later, David came to escort her to the dining room. She tucked her arm confidently into his, gathering the shimmering folds of her skirt in the other hand, radiating pride and happiness. A ripple of appreciation ran over the assembled guests, for David's rugged fairness complemented her dark and slender fragility.

'Such a handsome couple,' murmured the vicar's wife into Mrs Ramsay's ear. 'She seems a charming girl, you must be very pleased with your prospective daughter-in-law.'

'Indeed I am. And I'm glad to see David finally settle down—he's over thirty, you know. It's time he started a family of his own.'

Sara was never to forget her first formal dinner party in

David's home. The cook had excelled herself: French onion soup, thinly sliced smoked salmon, roast pheasant stuffed with wild rice, crêpes suzettes—each course was prepared to perfection. The wine glowed ruby-red in the fragile crystal as Dr Raymond, an old family friend, rose and proposed a toast: 'Sara and David, God bless them!'

The conversation was fluent—a heated political argument on her left, a knowledgeable discussion of the merits of a local artist on her right. In the lounge, coffee and liqueurs were served, and as she and David circulated around the room, Sara realised with an increasing sense of security that these witty and accomplished people were delighted by David's engagement, and very ready to welcome her into their circle.

After the last guest had left, she gratefully slid her aching feet out of their dainty silver sandals, and collapsed on to the brocaded sofa. David threw himself down beside her, grinning at her with his old familiar camaraderie.

'You were marvellous, Sara! A bit difficult to meet so many at once.'

'I even managed to call a few people by their right names!'

'John Raymond fell for you in a big way; I can see I'll have to keep my eye on you,' he teased.

Impudently she poked her tongue out at him, and he laughed at her comical look of dismay when his mother walked in the room in time to see her do it.

'Hello, my dears. I think everything went very well, don't you, David? Sara, you must be exhausted. Don't get up too early tomorrow, we mustn't send you back to work worn out.'

She smiled at them both, well content with the picture they made together, and not at all convinced that David didn't love this slip of a girl. Anyway, it wouldn't hurt to leave them alone. . . 'I can't take these late hours like I used to,' she said. 'Goodnight.'

When she had gone, David eyed his fiancée anxiously. 'She's right. I'm forgetting you still have your living to earn. Will you want to work after we're married, Sara?'

Elation at his concern welled up within her. She answered thoughtfully, 'I don't think so. It's more important I be here for Tim. He needs stability, and if I was away a lot, he wouldn't get it. Besides, I've worked hard ever since I left school—I might as well tell the truth, and admit I'm thoroughly looking forward to doing nothing for a change!'

A huge yawn took her unawares, and she blinked at him apologetically. 'I'm sorry, David. I assure you it's not your company. But I am tired, it's been quite a hectic day.'

She stood up and stretched unselfconsciously, her bare arms and shoulders pale against the heavy velvet. The vicissitudes of the evening had banished any constraint she might have felt in David's presence, and she was able to say honestly, 'Thank you for taking care of me so well this evening. I enjoyed meeting your friends.' She yawned again. 'Oh, dear, I've had it—I'll see you in the morning. Goodnight.'

He got to his feet, his eyes reminding her of his mother's in their gentleness. 'I'm going to have a last cigarette. Goodnight, Sara, pleasant dreams.' He made no attempt to kiss her, but his consideration enveloped her like a caress.

As the plane winged smoothly towards Saraguay, Sara sat with her eyes closed, endeavouring to sort out her impressions. The unknown had become the known, and in consequence was far less frightening; she felt much calmer about the future. She had an ally in David's mother and Tim was counting the days until she 'moved in', as he put it. Wistfully she twisted the sparkling ring on her finger. David was the only unpredictable factor. . . his feelings were as unreadable as the mysterious depths of the sapphire he had given her.

The remaining weeks of work flew by, the day came to make final goodbyes, and for the last time she closed the door of the little bungalow behind her. Prince was protestingly loaded into a metal cage and the two of them boarded the aircraft.

Sara was carrying a large box under her arm, not trusting the luggage compartment, for it contained her wedding dress. Some vestige of her independence had refused to allow her to patronise the expensive city bridal salons preferred by Mrs Ramsay. So she had shopped in Saraguay one Saturday, and to her pleased surprise had found a deliciously soft, pure white wool, as lightweight as gossamer. She had sewn it with long, bell-shaped sleeves, curved insets over the bust, and a straight fall of skirt to the floor. The finishing touch was a loose-fitting hood, lined with taffeta, which framed her dark hair with classic simplicity. It certainly wasn't everyone's idea of the typical wedding dress, but it satisfied Sara. She had remembered David's scathing comment about 'long white dresses', and was determined not to go up the aisle in yards of lace and tulle.

She and his mother had chatted on the phone several times since Sara's visit, for Mrs Ramsay insisted on leaving the major decisions to Sara—they were to be married in the evening by candlelight; Harold would give her away, Patricia would be her only bridesmaid. Due to the pressures of David's teaching schedule, the honeymoon had been postponed, to Sara's unspoken relief.

In spite of that, she had a full quota of pre-nuptial nerves as she descended from the plane. If only he loved her. . .if only she could be sure she was doing the right thing...thankfully she waved at David's tall figure, and with a minimum of fuss he loaded the car with the suitcases, her precious box, and an ecstatic dog.

'I thought for a while there was going to be a regular deputation to meet you—Stephen, Patricia and Tim were all set to come too!' he remarked, whipping out into the flow of traffic.

'I'm looking forward to seeing Marilyn and Harold again,' she replied, letting her eyes wander lovingly over his clean-cut features and shapely hands. In just over twenty-four hours she would be married to this man, a man whose deepest feelings were an enigma to her. It was a frightening thought, and she relapsed into silence, a silence intensified by the close confines of the car.

She was glad when they finally stopped in front of the house; David deputised the gardener to look after Prince, then escorted her into the spacious entrance hall, where a few short weeks ago she had greeted his guests. She fumbled with her gloves, gripped by a paralysing stage fright. How could she keep up this masquerade under the discerning eyes of Marilyn and Harold, who knew them both so well? With shaking fingers, she tried to undo her scarf.

'Let me do that, Sara,' David offered, his warm fingers brushing her chin. 'Cheer up, it's a wedding we're having tomorrow, not an execution!'

She raised grey eyes, dark with panic. An exclamation of mingled exasperation and amusement escaped him, and he enfolded her in a brotherly embrace, murmuring soothing bits of nonsense into her ear. For a moment she relaxed against him, her face buried in his shirt front, the warmth of his body seeping through the thin material.

'Better now?' he asked, and she nodded shamefacedly, grateful that he had understood her nervousness.

'Yes, thank you. I'm sorry about that.'

'You still look a bit funereal,' he drawled. 'We are engaged, remember, you're supposed to look happy.' He bent his head, still holding her shoulders, and kissed her firmly and thoroughly.

A rush of warm colour flooded her cheeks when Harold spoke behind them. 'That's enough, David! It's my turn to kiss the bride-to-be.'

Incoherently, she said, 'Harold, it's lovely to see you again. You're looking so well. And Marilyn, how are you?'

Her friend embraced her. 'Congratulations, Sara! We're all so happy for you. Patricia is in seventh heaven at the thought of being your bridesmaid.'

The two boys came running and pandemonium reigned. Dinner was a hilarious meal, for Harold was in top form and Marilyn delighted that her hopes for Sara had been realised; the three children became infected with the adults' excitement and had to be forcibly restrained. They all went to the brief rehearsal, after which David and Harold disappeared.

'Stag party,' Harold grinned. 'The groom's last fling!'

'Behave yourselves,' his wife jibed. 'Don't you dare be late at the church tomorrow.'

David winked impishly at his fiancée. 'How could I be, and she so beautiful!' he declined.

Marilyn need not have worried; the ceremony went off very smoothly.

Her wedding was to remain in Sara's memory in a series of sharp images: the peal of organ music that reverberated in the little stone chapel as she waited on Harold's arm; the glorious hues of the stained glass window behind the altar—peacock blue, blood-red, emerald, gold and amethyst; the deep peace which filled her when she pledged herself to David in the age-old promises—she loved him, and surely as they lived together from day to day, he would come to love her; the slight tremor in his hand as he slipped the plain gold band on her finger; the pure voices of the choir soaring to the vaulted ceiling; Patricia's elfin charm in her first long dress; the unashamed tears on Mrs Ramsay's cheeks; Tim's sober face after the mystery and wonder of the beautiful service.

Afterwards, at the city's most exclusive hotel, there were a formal dinner, complete with three-tiered cake and bubbling champagne. Sara was the traditional radiant bride, for, to her delight, David was continually at her side, his arm about her waist, his deep laugh matching her vivacious gaiety.

They cut the cake, Sara cautioning, 'Not all the way to the bottom, David, that's bad luck.' In the American way, he passed a tray of the dark fruit cake, she the light.

'I shall put it under my pillow tonight,' Patricia announced solemnly.

'That's girls' stuff,' Stephen scorned. 'I'm going to eat mine!'

'Keep the top layer for the christening,' added Dr Raymond mischievously, enjoying the bride's pink-cheeked confusion.

There were the usual toasts, then Harold read the telegrams, including one from Joan and Simon. For the benefit of the photographer, David gave her a lingering kiss, and recklessly she responded. Her heart was suffused with hope—could it be that, after all, theirs would be a true marriage from the beginning? Dared she believe it was not simply a cold-blooded marriage of convenience?

The moment came when they drove off together, in a shower of confetti, laughter and good wishes ringing in their ears. Sara leaned back against the soft leather upholstery with a contented sigh.

'We are lucky to have such good friends,' she said dreamily. 'Poor Harold was terribly nervous—he said Patricia would have to elope, he'd never be able to face that long aisle again!'

She looked over at her new husband, expecting an answering smile to light up his face. It came as a physical shock to see his features severe and withdrawn, his hands tense on the steering wheel. She must have made an involuntary sound of protest; he glanced at her with ice-blue eyes and said sardonically, 'Too much champagne? You'd better come down to earth again. I have to admit I'm glad that charade is over.'

Her eyes widened in incredulous pain; desperately she fought back silent tears, her fingers clenched in the delicate fabric of her wedding dress. So it had all been an act, a convincing performance, designed so his friends would not suspect he was anything but the normal, loving bridegroom. Of course, now that they were alone, there was no necessity for him to continue his impersonation. Deeply humiliated, she remembered how she had let her warm lips answer his kiss. How could she have been so silly! A host of bitter retorts sprang to her tongue, but she bit them back with a forlorn sigh—what was the use? What a fool she had been, thinking he had really meant those tender glances. . .

By the time they reached David's deserted house, she had a precarious grip on her emotions, and managed to say dispassionately, 'I'm tired, it's been a long day. I think I'll go to bed. Goodnight.'

Unable to meet his eyes, she walked upstairs with rigid dignity, praying that her self-control would last until she gained her room. She and David had adjoining bedrooms; she shut the door between them, before slowly taking off her white gown, and sliding between lavender-scented sheets. The hot tears could no longer be held back. She cried herself to sleep, her shining hopes reduced to desolate ashes.

CHAPTER TWELVE

THE SLOW autumn days crept by, reluctantly heralding the cold grip of winter. The maples dropped their cloaks of scarlet and yellow, lifting bare branches to the grey November skies. The roses were long gone; the relentless frosts had reduced the vivid chrysanthemums into withered brown skeletons, that rustled in the raw winds. A time of death, of nature sombre and melancholy, and spring too far away for hope. . .

Sara scuffled through a pile of shrivelled leaves; she had developed the habit of taking Prince for lonely walks in a nearby park every afternoon. Perhaps it was the time of year, she thought, but she was finding it increasingly difficult to maintain her characteristic optimism and serenity. Her marriage had fallen into a pattern, a pattern in which days would go by when she would scarcely see David at all. He left for the university early in the morning; they dined with Tim in the evening; then he frequently shut himself in his study, claiming he had essays to read or book reports to mark. He never forgot his impeccable good manners: he treated her with a distant politeness that made her feel like an unwanted stranger in his home.

Moreover, she had very little to occupy her time. The house ran on well-oiled wheels, and she could not deceive herself she was needed for its operation. The cook consulted her daily for any preference in menus—that was her sole contribution.

The only bright spot was Tim, the girl mused. He trusted her implicitly, for her continued presence was giving him the security and love he craved. She got him his breakfast, saw him off to school, and always had lunch with him. Together they raked up the leaves, made bonfires, and played with Prince. Gradually he started bringing school friends home, and Sara was touched by the pride in his voice as he introduced his 'new mother'.

Of course, on the credit side of her marriage, she had to admit David was most generous with his money—he gave her a monthly allowance which was more than adequate. For the first time in her life, she could indulge her very feminine love of beautiful clothes. And what fun it had been planting innumerable daffodils, tulips, crocuses and snowdrops without having to consider the cost!

But these advantages couldn't possibly compensate for the hurt that her husband's perfunctory attention caused her. He never touched her, and seemed to avoid any situation in which he might find himself alone with her. Since the disillusionment of her wedding night, the door between their adjoining rooms had remained shut; it seemed symbolic of the uneasy relationship between them, for in the same way David had shut her out from his companionship and laughter. In the long evenings, after Tim had gone to bed, she would find herself wondering with a sharp stab of jealousy whether he was writing to Linda behind those closed study doors. Now she knew how ridiculous had been her assumption that David would eventually fall in love with her.

She rarely even shared his leisure hours. Soon after their marriage, he had taken her down to the stables. He hadn't bothered hiding his irritation when she instinctively shrank from the stamping, curveting Arab mare he had wanted her to ride.

'I couldn't, David,' she had protested. 'I've never been on a horse in my life, and besides, I'm frightened of them. And they know it!' she added, trying to make him smile, as the mare wilfully blew down her neck.

He had not offered to teach her, nor had he requested her company to the stables again. On weekends, she would wistfully watch him ride off to the park astride a magnificent chestnut, he and the horse moving as one with a fluid grace she envied. So one morning, when the hours seemed to drag at a snail's pace, she defiantly pulled on a pair of old slacks and went to the tack room, with its rich odour of soft leather and last summer's hay.

'Good morning, ma'am,' the old groom greeted her, the burr of Devon in his speech.

'Could you teach me how to ride, Mr Hawkes?' she blurted, before her courage could desert her.

'Ah yes, I could indeed.' She darted a fearful glance at the aristocratic grey nose of the Arab mare. 'Not on that one,' he said calmly. 'She's kind, but too full of high spirits for you yet. Now Tara over here is gentle and slow, you'll get along fine together.'

Wisely he started her on stable chores, until she grew accustomed to moving around the bulky horses, and no longer jumped when they tossed their heads or swished their tails. The tenacity that had carried her through her therapy training she now applied to this new venture, and an undemanding friendship developed between her and old Bob Hawkes. It was a proud day for both of them when she and Tara walked, trotted, then cantered around the paddock.

'Don't tell my husband,' she requested breathlessly. 'I want to surprise him.' One entire wall of the stable was lined with cups and ribbons which David had won—she would never be in his class, but even if she could accompany him by next spring, it would be worth it.

So her riding lessons, walks with Prince and games with Tim came to fill her days, and the sharp agony of her initial disenchantment was blunted by the passage of time. She could recall only one incident when the barrier between her and David had been temporarily lowered. It had been about a week ago; they had been invited to Ruth and Gary Fielding's for a fondue, Gary being the newest member of David's staff. . .

The evening began disastrously with a near-quarrel before they left. Someone had tapped on her door while she was dressing; carelessly pulling on a négligé over her slip, she opened it, expecting one of the maids.

'Oh, it's you, David.' Hastily she belted the flimsy nylon gown about her waist.

'Help me with these studs, will you?' he asked impatiently. He bent his head and she pulled the tiny gold clasps through the collar, fastening his bow tie. He was so close she could smell the scent of his soap, and touch his thick hair, damp and unruly from the shower. Her fingers slipped; her fingernail dug into his neck and he jumped as though he had been stung. As one of the studs fell on the carpet and rolled under a chair, he glared at her in vexation.

Overwrought by the bittersweet emotions his nearness roused, she snapped, 'I'm sorry. Perhaps you'd better get one of the stable boys to help you. You spend more time down there than here, after all.'

His eye roved insolently around her bedroom. 'Spending time here wasn't part of the bargain, was it? Or are you changing your mind?'

She retreated, panic-stricken, feeling his eyes burn through the delicate gown. 'No. . .no, I'm not.' The grandfather clock sweetly chimed the hour; she said hurriedly, 'If I don't get ready, we'll be late.' She shut the door in his face, finishing her toilette with hands that shook. There were times when he seemed to hate her. . .

For the sake of her host and hostess, she bravely threw

off her depression. They were a likeable young couple, married less than a year—this was Gary's first job. Their flat was cramped and inconvenient, furnished with a haphazard assortment of second-hand pieces, but it was lit by a love and intimacy sadly lacking in David's elegant home.

Ruth Fielding was an X-ray technician; telling Sara about her job, she said, 'I'm working full-time, and we're trying very hard to bank every penny of my salary—we have our eye on an acre of land outside the city limits, we want to build our own house. Are you working, Mrs Ramsay?'

'Please do call me Sara. I'm still not used to answering to Mrs Ramsay! No, I'm not working. At the moment I think Tim—David's orphaned nephew—has priority over a job. His parents were killed three years ago, and he's very appreciative of the mothering I give him. Perhaps in a year or so I'll do some part-time physiotherapy.'

'It will be time then for a family of your own,' Ruth joked.

Sara blenched and shot an uncomfortable glance at David, who was fortunately engrossed in Gary's chess set. Realising she had said something wrong, Ruth kindly tried to put her beautiful guest at ease. 'We hope to wait a while. There's nothing I'd like more than a son or daughter, but Gary has debts from his years of studying, and we would like to have a garden and room for a child to play.'

Sara nodded in agreement and the awkward moment passed.

At the end of the evening, after Sara and David had thanked the Fieldings for their hospitality and said goodbye, Sara had turned back and seen them framed in the narrow doorway, Gary's arm around his wife's slender waist, her burnished auburn head resting confidently on his shoulder. She was very silent on the way home, unaware that David was observing the violet shadows under her eyes with concern.

He hung up her coat, detaining her with a hand on her elbow, and saying gently, 'You look tired, Sara. Are you feeling all right?'

His unaccustomed solicitude brought a lump to her throat. She replied stiffly, 'I have a headache, that's all.' It was true that the strain of appearing gay and lighthearted all evening had left her with a throbbing pain in her head.

'Go up to bed, I'll bring you a couple of aspirin,' he ordered, and too weary to argue, she did as she was told.

She was almost alseep when he entered; she sat up obediently and swallowed the pills, grimacing at their acrid flavour. Listless and detached, she lay back on the pillow. A vast lassitude had crept over her; she felt totally withdrawn from all the pain of the past few weeks. Tentatively he stroked her hair back from her forehead. 'I'm sorry I was irritable this evening. I'll get Tim off to school in the morning, you stay in bed,' she heard him say, before she succumbed to an exhausted sleep, her hand resting lifelessly in his.

But the next day, his closeness was only a memory, for he was as cool and remote as ever, and her life fell back into its quiet and often solitary routine. Consequently, one afternoon a couple of weeks later, she was only too pleased to have company on her ramble with Prince. She had just left the house when a sleek American car rolled down the drive, and a tall man climbed out. Incredulously, she recognised him.

'Charles!' she cried in delight, running across the lawn to meet him. 'How nice to see you again!'

He gave her a bear hug that almost lifted her off her feet, and surveyed her flushed and excited face. 'As beautiful as ever, I see. Marriage must be agreeing with you. Where are you going?'

'I'm taking the dog for his daily run. Why don't you come too!'

He tucked her arm sociably in his, and they set off to the park, deserted in the chill November wind. 'I'm here on business for three days,' Charles explained. 'I flew in from Toronto yesterday.'

He grinned at her, and she was amused to see a trace of embarrassment mar his habitual insouciance. 'I think I'm in love, Sara. She's a peach of a girl—the head secretary in the accounts department in my new office. Her name's Barbara, she's twenty-two, black-haired, beautiful, loves skiing and golf.'

'When are you going to put a ring on her finger?' Sara teased, happy that his unrequited summer romance had died a natural death.

'Soon, I hope. I haven't dared ask her yet.'

Sara chuckled. Barbara must be quite a girl, to rob Charles of his rather brash self-assurance!

Abruptly he stopped and she gazed at him in inquiry. 'Having trouble with that headstrong husband of yours?' he demanded.

Instinctively, she shook her head and he chided, 'Don't deny it, honey, it's standing out all over you.'

His rough sympathy was more than she could stand, and in spite of herself she began to cry. He put a comforting arm around her. 'Come on, tell me all about it. Begin at the beginning and don't leave anything out.'

After several false starts, the words came tumbling out—her friendship with David in July, their quarrel after the night on the island, David's romance with Linda, his strange proposal, the tensions of their artificial marriage. Finally she halted, fumbling for a handkerchief to wipe her wet cheeks. 'I guess I really needed a shoulder to cry on, didn't I?' she quavered.

'I don't know how you kept it to yourself this long. The trouble is, I feel partly responsible. I'm sure if I'd told David the reason why we were gone all night, you'd never have quarrelled and none of this would have happened.'

'Well, for heaven's sake, don't tell him now,' she said in alarm. 'I'll be OK.' She strived for a lighter note. 'If you promise not to say anything to him, you can come to our party tomorrow night. We're having a few friends in for drinks and a buffet supper around eight. Will you come?'

'Love to,' he agreed promptly; pleased, she forgot he had omitted his promise.

She didn't see David again until the following evening shortly before their party. Dressed in her long midnight blue velvet, she was busy supervising the last-minute details, when she heard his key in the lock and went to the door to meet him. How tired he looked! Timidly she murmured, 'You're working too hard, David.'

He glanced at her, his eyes dwelling on the lovely lines of her figure in the flowing velvet. 'Yes, I know. I'm in the middle of mid-term exams, it's always a hectic time. I'm sorry to be so late.'

Absurdly nervous, she went on, 'You'll never guess who I saw yesterday—I invited him to come tonight—Charles Rutherford. He's here on business for a few days.'

David frowned. 'What do you mean, you saw him yesterday?'

'He came to the house just as I was leaving with Prince, so we went for a walk in the park. He flies back to Toronto tomorrow night.'

His blue eyes bored into hers and he said cuttingly, 'It will be quite like old times for you, to have both of us dancing attendance on you.'

Conscious of a childish desire to strike back, she retaliated, 'All we need is Linda to make the foursome complete!'

He stepped towards her, tense with fury. To her infinite relief, she heard the housekeeper's footsteps entering the dining room, and fled ignominiously.

As their guests arrived, she hid her inner turmoil beneath a brittle gaiety, by which Charles, at least, was not deceived. She found his undemanding gallantry very soothing to her wounded ego; his ready wit made her laugh, temporarily oblivious of her troubles, and she spent the majority of the evening in his company. He was the last to leave, punctiliously thanking David for a pleasant evening, and quite openly kissing Sara goodbye.

'I'll get in touch next time I'm here, if I don't see you tomorrow,' he promised. 'Take care of yourself.'

The door closed behind him, and Sara said thoughtlessly, 'It was fun to see him again, wasn't it, David? I'd forgotten how nice he is.'

His reply stung her like a whiplash. 'Perhaps if he's so much fun, you should have married him rather than me!'

Uncomprehending, she said uncertainly, 'Don't be silly. I never wanted to marry him, we're just good friends—I suppose that sounds trite, but it's true.'

'It certainly didn't look that way to me this evening,' her husband interrupted furiously. 'Every time I turned around, the two of you had your heads together.'

'At least he pays me a little attention, which is more than you can be bothered to do,' she snapped, incensed. 'You're a dog in the manger, David. You don't want me yourself, but you won't let anyone else near me, either!'

In a towering rage, he grabbed her by the shoulders and pulled her towards him. 'Who told you I don't want you myself?' he grated.

Frantically she tried to resist him, but he was far too strong, and she was helpless in his cruel embrace. One hand at her waist, the other tangled in her silky hair, he kissed her, a long kiss of mingled bitterness and passion, which melted the bones in her body and sent a quiver of fire racing through her blood. With a violent gesture, he finally released her, his chest heaving. She heard him demand, 'Is that how your good friend Charles kisses you?'

Breathless and distraught, she lost the last scrap of her control, and all the pent-up tensions of their brief marriage exploded in a sob of anger. 'I hate you! I wish I'd never married you. Don't you ever touch me again!'

In a whirl of velvet skirts, she ran to her room, slammed the door and turned the key in the lock. The ugly words they had hurled at each other echoed in her ears, words that could never be recalled. The bright flame of her fury slowly sank and died, leaving her throat tight with pain, her eyes burning with unshed tears. She sat on the edge of the bed, trying to still the recurrent shivering of her limbs; scarcely aware of what she was doing, she began to brush her disordered hair.

By chance, her eyes fell on the painting David had given her—grey seas lashed the Point, spray flung high against a windswept sky. Nostalgia swept over her. Rocky Cape...the empty stretch of sand, the mew of gliding gulls, the thrust of spruce-clad hills into the cold Atlantic.

If I could walk along the beach and sit and watch the sea, she thought, perhaps I could sort all this out, and come to terms with it. I've got to do something, I can't go on like this. Strangely excited, she stared at her reflection in the mirror. I'll go, she decided. If I leave tomorrow after Tim goes to school, I can be there by mid-afternoon.

Worn out, she slept dreamlessly, and awoke with her decision unchanged. She gave Tim his breakfast, and packed him sandwiches to eat in school for lunch, explaining that she was driving to the Cape and would be home the next day. For she knew she would come back, if only to keep intact the love shining out of the boy's clear blue eyes. She couldn't betray that trust, no matter what David did. So when she kissed Tim goodbye, she promised, 'I'll see you tomorrow. Be a good boy.'

Packing was a simple matter of throwing a few warm clothes in a suitcase; the note to David took a little longer, but she settled for a brief statement of her plans, and dropped it in a prominent spot on the hall table. Prince clambered in the back seat and they were off.

She was driving David's second car, a Cadillac, and at first it took all her attention to cope with the unfamiliar controls in the city traffic. But she was soon on the open highway and drove steadily all morning, the miles accumulating between her and David, and the intolerable situation he represented. If it was escapism she was indulging in, she pondered, then a bit of escapism was long overdue, for she could feel her strained nerves relaxing already.

It was with a feeling of coming home that she parked under the big pine tree by David's summer house. Wet leaves carpeted the driveway and clogged the ditches. The scene was a study in the stark and sombre hues of late autumn—muted greys, browns and dark greens. The noisy summer birds had long fled south, leaving only the mournful sough of the wind uneasily swaying the branches of the evergreens.

Prince whined impatiently, so Sara climbed out of the car and let him out. Her legs were stiff and cramped, and her back ached from the long drive, but with new tranquillity, she could ignore this. The unmistakable tang of the ocean filled her nostrils, its distant rhythmic roar like sweet music in her ears.

She unlocked the door, unloading her suitcase and a few groceries in the kitchen, and set about preparing a late lunch. Then she changed into blue jeans and a heavy sweater, pulling on boots and her rain coat. A gaily patterned head-scarf and wool gloves against the November chill, and she was ready. She whistled to the dog, and together they ran down the path to the shore.

Her steps halted compulsively by the old spruce tree where she had literally bumped into David that long ago summer day—a violent beginning to a turbulent relationship, she thought wryly. Even then, had she been attracted to him, to his forceful personality, virile good looks and sinewy build?

On nimble feet, she scrambled over the rocks to the Point, searching for a spot sheltered from the raw wind. Hypnotised by the restless and ever-changing movements of the sea, she sat for a long time, her mind drifting as aimlessly as the strands of kelp in the tide. Eventually the chill penetrated her warm clothing, so she set off briskly down the beach, absorbed in memories of the precious companionship she had shared so briefly with David. She couldn't believe it had disappeared for ever; somehow it must be possible that they could live together in amity, if not in love.

It was only when she had picked her way across slime-covered rocks to a jagged cliff, and found it impassable, that she came out of her reverie, aware of the first twinges of disquiet. She had never come this far before. There was not a dwelling place or another human being in sight, while the melancholy screech of a herring gull overhead increased her sense of isolation. Ominous dark clouds had massed on the horizon and the light was rapidly fading.

Suddenly apprehensive, she called Prince, glad of his company, and turned back towards home. As she put a careless foot on a patch of slimy weed, her boot slipped. As she lost her balance, she felt a sickening wrench in her ankle. With a cry of pain she fell to her knees, lowering her head until the momentary waves of faintness and nausea had passed. Prince pushed his nose in her face, curious at her strange behaviour; Sara leaned her weight on him and tried to rise, but her injured foot would not support her, and again she collapsed on the wet stones.

Keep cool, she cautioned herself, don't panic. Remember your first aid training. Her usually clever fingers clumsy with cold, she probed the ankle. She was almost sure nothing was broken, just a bad sprain. To start with, she'd have to get above the tide mark. Painfully, on hands and knees, she crawled to the shelter of a cluster of boulders, rounded black shapes in the gloom. She sank back on the dry sand, clenching her teeth until the ache subsided.

The full extent of her predicament slowly dawned on her: no one knew where she was; she had not seen anyone on her walk, and the summer homes along the beach were all deserted. Furthermore, David wouldn't expect her home until tomorrow, she realised with a sick jolt of despair. Her jeans and the cuffs of her sweater were soaked, and she began to shiver uncontrollably, near tears. If she had to stay here all night, she would have pneumonia by morning, she thought grimly.

Prince whined, pulling at her coat, as anxious to be home as she was, and Sara bit her lip indecisively. He was her only hope—with cold fingers she tried to tie one of her water-soaked gloves around his collar. It didn't look particularly secure, so she reluctantly took off her silk scarf and knotted it firmly to the leather. 'Go and get help, Prince,' she commanded. 'Go!'

The dog regarded her with puzzled brown eyes, his head on one side, wishing his mistress would stop this foolish game—he wanted his supper. She slapped at him in exasperation, 'Go, Prince. Get help!'

Unwillingly he loped off into the gathering darkness, and was soon lost to sight. Surely he would find someone...if only she weren't so cold. The wind moaned around the looming blackness of the cliff; the gurgle and ripple of the advancing tide sounded sinister to her straining ears. The last vestige of light disappeared. Through scattered gaps in the clouds, a few stars twinkled impersonally.

Holding tight to her dwindling courage, she tucked her hands under her coat, and tried to pull up her knees for warmth, wincing with the pain. Eventually she fell into an uneasy doze, her head resting uncomfortably against the smooth rock surface, her body huddled on the sand.

She did not hear the scratch and patter of Prince's paws on the rocks; it was thus the man found her, her twisted body motionless, her face white in the torchlight. The dog gave a pleased whimper, as the man dropped to the ground beside her. She was convinced she was dreaming when she felt strong arms curve around her, and a beloved voice exclaimed 'Sara! Oh, sweetheart, I thought I'd never find you. What happened—are you all right?'

Bewildered, she blinked in the yellow glare of the torch. 'David?' she whispered. 'Oh, David, I was so frightened!' Tears of weakness trickled down her cheeks, and involuntarily she shuddered with cold.

He gathered her into a warm embrace against his broad chest. 'Hush, love, everything's all right. I've found you now and I'm never going to let you go. I love you so much, Sara. I think I died a thousand deaths the last couple of hours.'

Half laughing and half crying, she faltered. 'You love me?'

Her eyes widened in incredulous happiness at the utter sincerity of his reply. 'I think I've loved you ever since we met.'

Finally she could say the words that had been locked within her for five long months. 'I love you too, David.'

Somehow her arms were around his neck and he was kissing her, gently in the joy of their discovery, then with a deep and passionate hunger. Faint with ecstasy, she unthinkingly shifted her foot, and flinched at the shaft of pain that flamed through her ankle.

'What's the matter, darling?'

'I sprained my ankle. I don't know how I could have been so careless.' For the first time she noticed Prince waiting patiently in the background, tail wagging. 'I think he approves,' she giggled weakly. 'Thank heavens he found you. But when did you get here?'

'I followed you up to the Cape when I read your note. I've nearly been out of my mind with worry since I arrived and couldn't find you. I was just about ready to round up a search party when fortunately Prince had the sense to bark at the door. I recognised your scarf, and followed him here. And found the most wonderful welcome in the world,' he concluded tenderly. Their lips met again in lingering rapture.

Shyly she smiled at him, lost in an innocent wonder. 'I'm not dreaming, am I, David? I couldn't bear it if I was.'

'No, you're not dreaming. We love each other, and have the rest of our lives to prove it.'

Descending to practicalities, he chafed her icy hands in his. 'You're frozen, love, your clothes are soaked, and all I've done is kiss you!' Wrapping her in the thick blanket he had brought for just such an emergency, he effortlessly lifted her in his arms.

She was always to remember that journey home, David holding her close as though she were infinitely precious to him, occasionally dropping a kiss on her uplifted face, his voice rough with emotion as he talked.

'I went to the office as usual this morning, but I might as well have stayed home—I couldn't concentrate, all I could see was you, and all I could hear was your voice accusing me of not wanting you. Oh God, I've wanted you so much since we've been married, having you in the house all the time, knowing you were sleeping in the room next to mine. It's been hell, Sara. The only way I could cope was to keep you at a distance, a barrier between us. And, of course, to be out as much as possible.'

'Leaving me home crying because I thought you couldn't stand the sight of me,' Sara intervened. 'How stupid we've been!'

'We'll make up for it, sweetheart,' he promised, his laugh sure and happy in the darkness. 'Anyway, I went home for lunch today, and found your note—you said you were coming back tomorrow, but I didn't know whether to believe you or not. Then Charles dropped in—he was delayed for a day and wanted us to have dinner with him. I showed him your letter, after which he told me a few home truths: how worried he was about you, and what an idiot I was to neglect you so. He explained what happened the time you were gone all night.'

Abruptly he stopped, burying his face in her heavy hair with a groan of contrition. Lovingly she ran her fingers through his thick hair. How many times she had longed to do that!

Slowly he continued, 'You know Linda and I were engaged three years ago. I worshipped her, she dazzled and bewitched me so that I was completely blind to all her faults—and she had plenty of them. She never liked Tim and resented the time I spent with him. Once or twice I had to cancel dates with her because he was sick, or because I had to take him somewhere. Infatuated as I was, I knew she wasn't very pleased. Then I discovered she was seeing another man, and had even spent a weekend with him. I suppose my ideals are old-fashioned, but I was shattered to find she could behave like that. I accused her of being unfaithful—she was furious, told me if I wouldn't take her out, she certainly wasn't going to sit at home; and that if I wouldn't hand Tim over to his grandmother, she wouldn't marry me at all. We had a flaming row, she threw the ring in my face, and that was that. I'd idolised her to such an extent, it was a shock to see what she was really like. She made me very wary of the female sex.'

He stopped a moment, shifting the girl's body in his arms, a trace of moonlight illuminating the tenderness in his eyes. 'And then you came along into my well-ordered life—so innocent and untouched, so very different from Linda. I wanted to trust you, every instinct I possessed told me to trust you. But when you were gone with Charles that night, it was like a repetition of the affair with Linda, and I guess I lost my head. I was desperately sorry afterwards, but by then you and Charles seemed to have paired off. It was sheer perversity that made me go out with Linda again. I felt at such a loose end, because I'd decided you must be in love with Charles. You never were, were you, sweetheart?'

'No, never. It was always you, right from the beginning.'

His arms tightened around her. 'Then why did you back off every time I tried to touch you?'

'Oh, David,' she laughed, 'because I wanted so much

to respond, but I thought you only married me to get a glorified housekeeper! I had my pride too, you know.'

She hid her flushed face in his rough jacket. The chill had gone from her body, and more important, from her heart. Always she would be enfolded in the passion and steadfastness of his love.

He stumbled over a clump of grass, and she looked up in surprise at the house outlined against the sky. 'Why, we're home.'

'Yes, we're home,' David repeated, a wealth of love in the simple words. 'I didn't carry you over the threshold on our wedding day, did I? But tonight, I will. Welcome home, my beautiful Sara. Welcome home for ever.'

Mills & Boon

Next month's Romances

Each month, you can chose from a world of variety in romance with Mills & Boon. These are the new titles to look out for next month.

ONCE BITTEN, TWICE SHY ROBYN DONALD
SAVING GRACE CAROLE MORTIMER
AN UNLIKELY ROMANCE BETTY NEELS
STORMY VOYAGE SALLY WENTWORTH
A TIME FOR LOVE AMANDA BROWNING
INTANGIBLE DREAM PATRICIA WILSON
IMAGES OF DESIRE ANNE BEAUMONT
OFFER ME A RAINBOW NATALIE FOX
TROUBLE SHOOTER DIANA HAMILTON
A ROMAN MARRIAGE STEPHANIE HOWARD
DANGEROUS COMPANY KAY GREGORY
DECEITFUL LOVER HELEN BROOKS
FOR LOVE OR POWER ROSALIE HENAGHAN
DISTANT SHADOWS ALISON YORK
FLORENTINE SPRING CHARLOTTE LAMB

STARSIGN
HUNTER'S HAREM ELEANOR REES

Available from Boots, Martins, John Menzies, W.H. Smith, most supermarkets and other paperback stockists.

Also available from Mills & Boon Reader Service, P.O. Box 236, Thornton Road, Croydon, Surrey CR9 3RU.

ESPECIALLY FOR YOU ON MOTHER'S DAY

OUT OF THE STORM - Catherine George
BATTLE FOR LOVE - Stephanie Howard
GOODBYE DELANEY - Kay Gregory
DEEP WATER - Marjorie Lewty

Four unique love stories beautifully packaged, a wonderful gift for Mother's Day - or why not treat yourself!

Published: February 1992   Price: £6.40

*Available from Boots, Martins, John Menzies, W.H. Smith, most supermarkets and other paperback stockists.
Also available from Mills & Boon Reader Service, PO Box 236, Thornton Road, Croydon, Surrey CR9 3RU.*

Mills & Boon

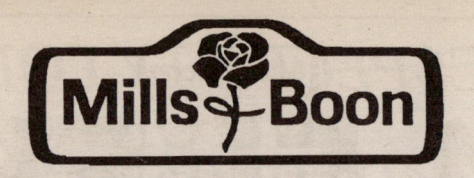

Forthcoming Titles

COLLECTION
Available in February

The Betty Neels Collection — **AT THE END OF THE DAY**
NEVER THE TIME AND THE PLACE

The Patricia Wilson Collection — **A MOMENT OF ANGER**
BRIDE OF DIAZ

BEST SELLER ROMANCE
Available in March

DESIRES CAPTIVE Penny Jordan
NO MANS POSSESSION Sophie Weston

MEDICAL ROMANCE
Available in March

DEMPSEY'S DILEMMA Christine Adams
WIND OF CHANGE Clare Lavenham
DOCTOR ON SKYE Margaret O'Neill
CROSSROADS OF THE HEART Judith Worthy

Available from Boots, Martins, John Menzies, W.H. Smith, most supermarkets and other paperback stockists.

Also available from Mills & Boon Reader Service, P.O. Box 236, Thornton Road, Croydon, Surrey CR9 3RU.

Readers in South Africa - write to:
Book Services International Ltd, P.O. Box 41654, Craighall, Transvaal 2024.

4 FREE

Romances and 2 FREE gifts just for you!

You can enjoy all the heartwarming emotion of true love for FREE! Discover the heartbreak and the happiness, the emotion and the tenderness of the modern relationships in Mills & Boon Romances.

We'll send you 4 captivating Romances as a special offer from Mills & Boon Reader Service, along with the chance to have 6 Romances delivered to your door each month.

Claim your FREE books and gifts overleaf...

An irresistible offer from Mills & Boon

Here's a personal invitation from Mills & Boon Reader Service, to become a regular reader of Romances. To welcome you, we'd like you to have 4 books, a CUDDLY TEDDY and a special MYSTERY GIFT absolutely FREE.

Then you could look forward each month to receiving 6 brand new Romances, delivered to your door, postage and packing free! Plus our free newsletter featuring author news, competitions, special offers and much more.

This invitation comes with no strings attached. You may cancel or suspend your subscription at any time, and still keep your free books and gifts.

It's so easy. Send no money now. Simply fill in the coupon below and post it to -
Reader Service, FREEPOST, PO Box 236, Croydon, Surrey CR9 9EL.

------- NO STAMP REQUIRED -------

Free Books Coupon

Yes! Please rush me my 4 free Romances and 2 free gifts! Please also reserve me a Reader Service subscription. If I decide to subscribe I can look forward to receiving 6 brand new Romances each month for just £9.60, postage and packing free. If I choose not to subscribe I shall write to you within 10 days - I can keep the books and gifts whatever I decide. I may cancel or suspend my subscription at any time. I am over 18 years of age.

Name Mrs/Miss/Ms/Mr _____ EP18R

Address _____

_____

Postcode _____ Signature _____

Offer expires 31st May 1992. The right is reserved to refuse an application and change the terms of this offer. Readers overseas and in Eire please send for details. Southern Africa write to Book Services International Ltd, P.O. Box 41654, Craighall, Transvaal 2024.
You may be mailed with offers from other reputable companies as a result of this application.
If you would prefer not to share in this opportunity, please tick box. ☐